I0639464

Thomas Major

The ruins of Pæstum otherwise Posidonia, in Magna Græcia

Otherwise Posidonia, in Magna Græcia

Thomas Major

The ruins of Pæstum otherwise Posidonia, in Magna Græcia
Otherwise Posidonia, in Magna Græcia

ISBN/EAN: 9783741181184

Manufactured in Europe, USA, Canada, Australia, Japa

Cover: Foto ©Andreas Hilbeck / pixelio.de

Manufactured and distributed by brebook publishing software
(www.brebook.com)

Thomas Major

The ruins of Pæstum otherwise Posidonia, in Magna Græcia

THE

RUINS

OF

PÆSTUM,

OTHERWISE

POSIDONIA,

IN

MAGNA GRÆCIA.

By *THOMAS MAJOR*, Engraver to His Majesty.

LONDON:

Publifhed by T. Major, in *St. Martin's Lane.*

Printed by James Dixwell, MDCCLXVIII.

TO HIS GRACE

GEORGE *Duke of* MONTAGU,

MARQUIS of MONTHERMER,

EARL of CARDIGAN, &c. &c.

With the utmost Gratitude and Respect this BOOK is humbly INSCRIBED,

By HIS GRACE's

Most dutiful and obedient Servant,

THOMAS MAJOR.

Subfcribers to the Ruins of *Pæftum*.

The KING.

His Majefty the KING of POLAND.

His Royal Highnefs the DUKE of GLOUCESTER.
His Royal Highnefs the DUKE of CUMBERLAND.

A

THE Right Hon. the Earl of Afhburnham
The Right Hon. the Earl of Albemarle
Robert Adair, Efq;
William Adair, Efq;
The Rev. Mr. John Alleyne, Univerfity College, Oxford, 2 Books
Mark Akenfide, M. D. Phyfician to Her Majefty
Abraham Atkins, Efq;

B

The Right Hon. Lord Bruce
The Right Hon. Lord Beauchamp
The Hon. Mr. B. Bathurft
James Bindley, Efq; 4 Books
Thomas Brand, Efq; of the Hyde, Effex
Thomas Brand, Efq; of the Hoo, Hertfordfhire
William Blair, Efq;
Henry Bullock, Efq;
Jacob Elefquiere, Efq;
John Barnard, Efq;
John Bell, Efq;
Richard Bull, Efq;
Robert Bromfield, M. D.
John Brettell, Efq;
The Rev. Mr. Phanuel Bacon, D. D.
Thomas Birch, Efq; of Hatton Garden
William Bayntun, Efq; of Gray's Inn

C

The Right Hon. Lord Camden, Lord High Chancellor of Great Britain
The Right Hon. the Earl of Charlemont
The Right Hon. Lord Frederic Cavendifh
The Right Hon. Lord John Cavendifh
John Comyns, Efq;
Auguftus Crews, Efq;
William Caftle, Efq;
Major General Caillaud
William Chambers, Efq; Architect to His Majefty
John Campbell, Efq;
Charles Chauncy, M. D. 6 Books
Mr. Robert Clee, Engraver
Mr. Thomas Clark, Plaifterer to his Majefty
Mr. Chapman, Plumber
William Caflon, Efq; Letter Founder
Charles Chefter, Efq;

D

The Hon. and Right Rev. the Lord Bifhop of Durham
Matthew Duane, Efq; 2 Books
Peter Delme, Efq; 2 Books
Henry Dawkins, Efq;
Francis Darourre, Efq;
James Dickfon, Efq;
Thomas Dundas, Efq;
Bartholomew Dixon, Efq;
The Rev. Mr. Dampier, D. D. Eton College
The Rev. Mr. Dixon
Mr. Jofeph Dixon, Mafon
Mr. Dodfley, Bookfeller, 6 Books

E

The Right Hon. the Earl of Exeter, 4 Books

The Right Hon. Welbore Ellis, Efq; 2 Books
Mr. John Ellis, Attorney
Thomas Eyres, Efq;
William Benfon Earl, Efq;
Mr. Peter Elmfly, Bookfeller, 4 Books

F

Sir Robert Foley, Bart.
William Fouquier, Efq;
Thomas Falconer, Efq; at Chefter
Theodofius Forreft, Efq;

G

His Excellency Sir James Gray, Bart. Knight of the Bath, His Majefty's Ambaffador Extraordinary and Plenipotentiary at Madrid.
Major General Gray
Major General Ganfell
Mrs. Griffiths, Abingdon Buildings
Mr. Ifaac Goffet, jun. B. A. of Exeter College, Oxford
Mr. Herbert Gomond, Engraver.
Mr. Paul Garron, Engraver
Mr. Greenel, Builder

H

The Right Hon. the Earl of Hardwicke
The Right Hon. the Earl of Holdernefs
The Right Hon. the Earl of Hertford
Thomas Hollis, Efq;
Timothy Hollis, Efq;
Edward Horne, Efq; 3 Books
Thomas Hervey, jun. Efq;
———— Hodgkinfon, Efq;
George Hardinge, Efq;
William Hallet, Efq; of Canons
William Hunter, M. D. Phyfician to Her Majefty
The Rev. Mr. Richard Harrifon
Mr. Samuel Harding
Mr. Francis Hiron, of Warwick, Architect

J

Edmond Jennings, Efq; of Lincoln's Inn
Thomas Jones, Efq;
Mr. Richard Jupp, jun. Surveyor

K

The Hon. Admiral Keppel
R. Knight, Efq;
John Kenrick, Efq; 2 Books
Thomas King, Efq;
The Rev. Mr. Kaye
Chriftopher Kelly, M. D.
Mr. Edward Knight
Mr. Knight

L

The Right Hon. Lord Le Defpencer
The Right Rev. the Lord Bifhop of Lincoln
Mifs A. B. Ledien, of Reading
The Rev. Mr. Lort, Trinity College, Cambridge
Edmond Le Grand, Efq;
Emanuel Lutterloh, Efq;
John Longfield, M. D.
John Lockman, Efq;

M

His Grace the Duke of Montague

SUBSCRIBERS to the RUINS of PÆSTUM.

Her Grace the Duchess of Montague
The Right Hon. the Marquis of Montheriner
The Right Hon. the Earl of Morton, President of
    the Royal Society
The Right Hon. Humphry Morrice, Efq;
Edward Mason, Efq;
Matthew Maty, M. D.
John Monro, M. D.
James Martin, Efq;
Charles Mellifh, Efq;
Samuel Moore, Efq;
Richard Milles, Efq;
Robert Mylne, Efq; Architect
Mr. Frederick Miller
Mr. John Millan, Bookfeller, 6 Books

N
His Grace the Duke of Northumberland
Peter Nouaille, Efq; 2 Books
Mr. William Newton, Architect

O
William Oliver, Efq;

P
His Grace the Duke of Portland
The Right Hon. Lord Vifcount Palmerfton
The Hon. Mr. Proby
Governor Pownal
Samuel Pechel, Efq; Mafter in Chancery
Thomas Pratt, Efq;
Thomas Pennant, Efq;
The Rev. Mr. Pilkington, Magdalen College, Oxford
Mr. Parker, Printfeller, 2 Books

R
The Moft Noble the Marquis of Rockingham, 2 Books
The Hon. Mr. Thomas Robinfon
Sir Thomas Robinfon, Bart.
Charles Rogers, Efq;
Captain S. Riou, Canterbury

S
The Right Hon. the Earl of Shelburn, one of His
    Majefty's Principal Secretaries of State
Andrew Stone, Efq; Treafurer of Her Majefty's
    Houfhold, 3 Books
Charles Selwin, Efq;
John Sargent, Efq;
Captain John Sivright
John Smith, Efq; of Sudling, Dorfetfhire
J. Chriftopher Smith, Efq;
William Sheldon, Efq;
Thomas Sandby, Efq;
The Rev. Mr. Southgate
Mr. James Stephen, Surgeon
Mr. Thomas Smith, Painter
Mr. Shropfhire, Bookfeller
Mr. Snelling, Bookfeller

T
The Right Hon. Lord Trevor
The Rev. Mr. Totton, at Edgware
Robert Thompfon, Efq;
Boyce Tree, Efq;
Thomas Townfend, Efq;
Mr. ——— Tuckfield

U
Francis Villion, Efq;
William Villebois, Efq;
Robert Udny, Efq;

W
The Right Hon. the Earl of Waldegrave

The Right Rev. the Lord Bifhop of Worcefter
The Right Hon. the Lord Chief Juftice Willmot
Sir Watkin Williams Wynn, Bart.
Robert Wood, Efq; 6 Books
Elbro Woodcock, Efq;
Saunders Welch, Efq;
Jofeph Wilton, Efq; Sculptor to His Majefty
The Rev. Dr. Wetherell, Mafter of Univerfity College,
    Oxford
Mr. Michael White
Mr. Weft, of Deptford
Mr. William Webley, Chancery Lane
Mr. Henry Webley, Bookfeller
Mr. Walter, Bookfeller

Y
His Excellency Sir Jofeph Yorke, Knight of the Bath,
    His Majefty's Ambaffador, &c. at the Hague
The Hon. Mr. John Yorke
The Hon. and Rev. Mr. James Yorke, Dean of Lincoln

PUBLIC LIBRARIES.
Oxford.
Magdalen College
Univerfity College
Corpus Chrifti College
Trinity College
All Souls College

Cambridge.
Trinity College
Bennet's College
Caius College

FOREIGN SUBSCRIBERS.
PARIS.
Monf. J. G. Soufflot, Chevalier de l'Ordre du
    Roy, Control. des Bat. du Roy a Paris. M. de
    L'A. R. d' Archit.
Monf. Le Roy; Hiftoriogr. de l'L. A. R. d' Archit.
Monf. Godefroy de Villetaneufe
Monf. L'Abbé Barthelemy de l'Acad. Roy. des Infer.
    Garde des Medailles & Antiques de S. M. T. C. &c.
Monf. P. Marriette
Monf. P. Rémy, Peintre, ancien Directeur de l'Acad.
    de St. Luc, à Paris
Mad. Marie Anne Victoire Le Maignant
Monf. Elie de Beaumont, Confeiller au Parlement
Monf. Le Blanc
Monf. Joullain, 2 Books
Monf. Petit

Sir Theodore de Smeth, Barns of Deurne and Lieffel,
    Lord of Alphen and Rietveld, old Prefid.
    Alderman of the City of Amfterdam
Monf. P. Fouquet, jun. Painter, Amfterdam
M. Cornelius Ploos van Amftel, C. z. Amfterdam
Mr. John Enfchede, Letter Founder and Printer,
    at Haerlem
Rich. Wolters, Efq; His Majefty's Agent, at Rotterdam
Monf. Henri Fagel, Secretaire de L. LH. H. P. P. les
    Etats Generaux des Provinces Unies
Petrus Camper, Med. & Chir. & Botan. Profeffor
    in Acad. Groningo-Omlandica Ordin. F. R. S.
    Edenburgenfis Societ. Holland. quæ Hurtenal eft,
    nec non Acad. Reg. Chirurg. Parifienfis. Socius.
Monf. Francis Mollis, Antwerp
Paul Gavers, Efq; Director of the Weft India
    Company at Rotterdam
Mr. Jacob Garron, at Lifbon
Monf. Schreger, Berlin

To the R E A D E R.

OF all the Nations of Antiquity, the *GREEKS* may juftly claim the Superiority, as they furnifh Hiftory with precious Monuments and illuftrious Atchievements; whether we confider the Glory of their Arms, the Wifdom of their Laws, or their other Accomplifhments: Every Circumftance concurred to render *Greece* a School for the reft of Mankind. The Graces delighted in this Spot, and the Arts, Sciences, and Philofophy, feemed to vye with each other, which fhould moft ornament and improve it; nay, it may be faid to have been the Center, where every Ray of Learning and Wifdom was united, which at that Time humanized and embellifhed the World. Therefore it is impoffible not to be interefted in favour of fuch a People, efpecially, fince their remarkable Actions have been tranfmitted down to us by Authors of the firft Rank and Abilities; Men who diftinguifhed themfelves by their Military Exploits, as well as by their Writings, and were as great Commanders and Politicians, as excellent Hiftorians. In the fhort Space of little more than a Century, they arrived to the higheft Degree of Perfection in Painting, Sculpture, and Architecture, that we can fcarce help confidering this Age as the Golden Period. This naturally raifes in us a Curiofity to fearch into the Rife and Progrefs of fo illuftrious a People; and, with refpect to the firft, the Engraver hopes the prefent Work will fully fhew the State of *Grecian* Architecture in its Infancy, and from thence we may trace the Steps of its progreffive Improvements, to that Elegance, Grandeur and Magnificence, which have been the Admiration of the fucceeding Ages; and this Curiofity may be amply fatisfied, by confulting the feveral very exact Reprefentations of the noble Remains of Antiquity (1), which have been received by the Public, with the Applaufe that ever attends, and is the trueft Criterion of fuch excellent Performances.

THE City of *Pæftum*, or *Pofidonia*, whofe Remains are here exhibited, hath been, 'till very lately, almoft buried in Oblivion. The Caufes of the Depopulation of *Magna Græcia* extending to this City, have, for many Ages, rendered its Territories a Defert, unfrequented by the adjacent Inhabitants, and little known to Travellers. However, within thefe few Years, this Place has been vifited by the Curious; and among others, by an *Englifh* Gentleman, to whom the following Work owes its Birth; and who procured at *Naples* feveral fine Drawings of thefe Temples. The other Views were taken in Prefence of his Excellency Sir JAMES GRAY (2), whilft His Majefty's Envoy Extraordinary and Plenipotentiary at the Court of *Naples*. The Plans, Elevations, and Meafures, the Public owe to that eminent Artift, Monf. J. G. SOUFFLOT (3): They were by him accurately taken on the Spot (4), and he has generoufly affifted the Engraver in this Undertaking.

---

(1) The Ruins of *Palmyra*, 1753, and *Balbec*, 1757, by M. WOOD and DAWKINS. *Les Ruines des plus beaux Monuments de la Grece*, 1758, by M. LE ROY. The Antiquities of *Athens*, by M. STUART and REVETT, 1762, &c.

(2) Bart. Knight of the Bath, Appointed His Majefty's Ambaffador at the Court of *Spain*, in 1767.

(3) Knight of the Order of ST. MICHAEL, Architect to His moft *Chriftian* Majefty, Member of the Royal Academy of Architecture, and Controller of *Paris*.

(4) See LE ROY, *Monum. de la Grece. Difcours fur l'Hiftoire de l'Architecture Civile*, Page X, Note (b).

Thus

Thus furnished with Materials, and not knowing that any Attempts of this Kind, in several detached Pieces, had been made by others, the Engraver was induced to believe that this Performance, from the singular Construction of the Edifices, would prove acceptable to the Public. These Temples are esteemed by the learned as some of the most curious Remains of Grecian Antiquity, the most entire of any now existing, and are noble Monuments of the Magnificence of that ancient City.

This Work is divided into three Parts. The first contains a summary Account of the Origin of Pæstum, or Posidonia, and likewise of its ancient and modern State: The second, a Description of the Temples, with some occasional Remarks thereon: The third is a Dissertation upon the Coins and Medals of that City. As no Attention or Expence have been spared to render this Work as complete as possible, the Engraver hopes this Performance will be received with Indulgence. For the Illustration of the Prints, and Historical Account, he has availed himself of whatever could be gathered from various Authors who have treated on this Subject; and how far he has succeeded, is left to the Determination of the Public; to whom he begs leave to express his grateful Acknowledgements, for the favourable Reception hitherto bestowed upon his Labours.

For the Conveniency of Foreigners, he has given a Translation of this Work in French: And he takes this Occasion of expressing his Gratitude to the French Nation, for the many Civilities and Instructions he has received from their Artists, notwithstanding the Affair which happened to him while he was pursuing his Studies at Paris (1).

And here, he cannot but observe with Pleasure, the great Improvements (the Effect of generous Encouragement) that his Countrymen have made in the several Branches of Art. Their Productions, particularly in Painting and Engraving, so generally approved at the annual public Exhibitions, sufficiently refute invidious Reflections sometimes thrown on them, that their chief Efforts center in Schemes of raising a Fortune: and also the unfavourable Opinion, entertained by some Foreigners (2), of the Abilities of the English Artists. If we consider the Disadvantage they labour under, of not having hitherto had any Public Academy; and of being, for the most Part, obliged to complete their Studies abroad; it is rather to be wondered that they have made so great a Progress; and is a convincing Proof of the natural Strength of English Genius, not less capable of distinguishing itself in the liberal Arts, than in the most abstruse Sciences.

London, June, 1767.

(1) The Engraver, with others of his Countrymen, was confined in the Bastile in 1746, by way of Reprisal for the French and Irish Soldiers, taken Prisoners by the English; but was released in ten Days by that generous Protector of Arts, the Marquis d'Argenson, Minister of State for Foreign Affairs.

(2) Particularly the Translator of the learned Abbé Winkelman's Histoire de l'Art chez les Anciens, Tom. I. P. ii. French Edition, Amsterdam, 1766.

Tab. XXVI.

E N Q U I R Y

I N T O T H E

ORIGIN and Ancient STATE

O F

POSIDONIA, or *PÆSTUM*.

MONG the innumerable Evils, of which the diabolical Rage for War is productive, it is perhaps none of the leaft, that the Attention of the Hiftorian is fo engroffed by the Battles and Exploits of Heroes, that thofe Benefactors to Mankind, who have figured in Arts or Sciences, and employed all their Time and their Talents in civilizing the World, are either entirely forgot, or confidered only as acting an under Part on the great Stage of Life. Whoever confiders the noble Remains of Art, exhibited in the following Sheets, muft conclude, that the City, which contained them, did once make a very confiderable Figure; and argue by analogy, that the fame Tafte and Skill, which were exerted in raifing thefe Buildings, were not confined to Architecture only, but produced a fimilar Excellence in the whole Circle of Arts and Sciences: So that *Pofidonia*, in thefe Particulars, might once perhaps have been not much inferior to *Athens* itfelf: And yet fo it is, that very fcanty Materials for its Hiftory are to be found in the ancient Writers, by whom, when we have

C

been

been told that it was fuccessively possessed by the *Darians*, the *Sybarites*, the *Lucanians* and the *Romans*, we shall have learned the chief of what they have been pleased to inform us. However, we will endeavour to glean from them what we can upon the Subject, and supply the Defects by some Particulars of the neighbouring *Græcian* States in *Italy*; all of which, though independent of one another as to Government, yet agreed in Language, in Customs and in Manners; being all of them Colonies at different Times from *Old Greece*; who, possessing themselves of the Sea-Coasts of *Italy*, drove the ancient Inhabitants into the inland Parts; of whom also, and of the Country they inhabited, it may be necessary to premise some short Account.

What is now called *Italy* went originally by several Names. So Virgil informs us (1)

And the Saturnian *Land oft chang'd its Name.*

On which his Commentator Servius remarks, that it was called *Ausonia, Hesperia, Saturnia* and *Vitalia:* The latter from *Italus*, the Leader of a Colony; but as Varro (2) suppofes from *Vituli*, the Cattle which were found in great Numbers by the first Settlers. It was probably peopled, soon after the Dispersion, by some of those Wanderers from the *East*, who ranging the *Mediterranean* Sea, settled upon its Coasts and Islands, as far as *Hercules' Pillars*. Those who came to *Italy* we find distinguished by the Names of *Umbri, Siculi, Sabini, Aufones, Opici,* or *Osci*. The old Inscriptions which are found in *Italy* in different Languages and Characters from the *Greek* and *Latin*; the old Names of Towns, which can be reduced to no *Greek* nor *Latin* Etymology, and which, being explained from the *Oriental* Languages, agree well with many Circumstances of their History and Situation, pretty clearly shew from whence we must derive the ancient Inhabitants. Of those, before mentioned, Strabo fays, that the *Sabins* were to be reckoned among the Oldest and *Aborigines*; that from these were derived the *Picentins* and *Samnites*, from whom came the *Lucanians*, and from these the *Brettians* (3).

Long after these, a great Number of Colonies from *Greece*, under various Leaders, took Possession of all the Sea-Coasts of *Italy*, driving the original Inhabitants, whom they called by one common Name (4) *Barbarians*, into the Μεσογαια, or Inland Parts, established themselves, built flourishing Cities, and for a considerable Space of Time made a very distinguished Figure in Science, in Arts and in Arms; insomuch that they had the

---

(1) Sæpius & memori pectoli Saturnia **Tellus**.

Æn. VIII. 329.

(2) *Italia* a vitulis dicta ut dicit **Piso.**

R. R. 2. 1. 9.

And again,

Græcia antiqua ut scribit *Timæus* **Tauros** vocabant Βους, a quorum multitudine & pulchritudine & fœtu vitulorum *Italiam* dixerunt.

R. R. 2. 5. 3. The *Itali* fignorum profuso, would restore *Italia* to its old Pronunciation.

(3) Εν δε καταλεγειν χρη δι Σαβινι και Αβοριγινες, τουτων Πικεντινι και Σαμνιτικι, δυτων δι Λυκανοι, τουτων δι Βρεττιοι.

L. V. 218.

(4) The Name *Barbarian* was originally not so much a Term of Reproach but of Distinction only; under which the *Greeks* included all those Nations that did not inhabit *Old Greece*, or were Colonies from thence.

το *Βαρ* in the *Oriental* Languages fignifies that Part of a Country which is distant from a Dwelling or Town, a Champion, a Desert; the Word being doubled, according to the Idiom of those Languages is brought to fignify, One that lives at a great Distance, a Stranger, or Foreigner, a Person of a different Country and Language, in which Sense Ovid speaks of himself in his Banishment at *Pontus*,

Barbarus hic ego sum quia non intelligor ulli.

Trist. V. 1.

But afterwards the Contract between the *Greeks* and other Nations, as to Politeness and Civility, because so strong, that *Barbarian* grew to be synonimous with rude and savage; by somewhat the same Progress have our *English* Words *Knave* and *Villain* become Terms of Reproach.

Vanity to diftinguifh the Country they had taken Poffeffion of by the Name of *Magna Græcia* (1).

AMONG the principal Colonies from *Old Greece* fettled here, were the *Crotonians*, the *Locrians*, the *Sybarites*, the *Caulonians*, the *Metapontins* and the *Tarentins*; who, as they came here independent of one another, fo they continued; and encreafing daily in Wealth and Luxury, in the latter of which they feemed to have exceeded the moft debauched *Afiatic* Court, they naturally fell into Rivalfhips, Jealoufies, Quarrels and bloody Wars (2); and the Confequence of thefe was, the *Barbarians* falling upon, and revenging themfelves by Plunder and Slaughter for the Lofs of the better Parts of their ravifhed Territories; whilft the *Romans* ftood by and enjoyed the Storm; and when they had fufficiently weakened each other, feized the Opportunity of crufhing them all; making them dependent, in a greater or lefs Degree, on the City of *Rome*. The Language, Laws and Cuftoms of the *Greek* Cities, were by Degrees exchanged for thofe of *Rome*, and the Name of *MAGNA GRÆCIA*, which, with an infulting Air of Triumph over their Mother-Country, they had given to their new acquired Territories, gave Place to the ancient Name of *Italy* (3).

IN a Part of *Italy*, having the River *Silarus* on the Weft, the *Lucanian* Mountains on the Eaft, and the *Pofidonian* Bay on the South, and in the Middle of this Bay was the City *Pofidonia*, or *Pæftum*, fituated: of its Origin, the only Account we have given us in the ancient Writers, is by SOLINUS, who fays that it was built by the *Dorians*, (4) and thefe have been generally fuppofed to have come hither from *Old Greece:* But an ingenious modern Writer, in a very learned Work lately publifhed, (5) has taken upon him to prove, that thefe *Dorians* came directly hither from the *Eaft*, and made a Settlement as

---

(1) Ipfi de eâ (fc. *Italia*) judicaverunt *Graci*, genus in gloriam fuam effufiffimum, quotam partem ex eâ appellando *Graeciam Magnam*, PLINI; Hift. L. III. c. 5. It is not only to fhut out from the ancient Authors when, or upon what Occafion, this Appellation was given to *Italy*, nor to how large a Part of it, HERODOTUS makes Ufe of another Expreffion for it, having Occafion to fpeak of the *Crotonians* that affifted at the Battle of *Sebaris*, he fays, Το̃ δὲ ΕΚΤΟΣ τῆϛ μεγάληϛ Κροτωνίηϛ μοῦνος ἴηϛ ὁ Κολοφώνιοϛ ἐξ ἑαυτοῦ αὐθέντηϛ. VIII. 47. And in POLYBIUS's Time it had ceafed to be called fo; for, mentioning the Burning of the *Pythagorean* Colleges, he fays, Ἐν ἴαϛ κατὰ τὴν Ἰταλίαν τότε καλουμένην ΜΕΓΑΛΗΝ ΕΛΛΑΔΑ ΤΟΤΕ προϛαγορευομένην. 2. P. 175. SERVIUS, on the 1ft. Æn. 573, fays, *Italia Magna Ellas*, id eft, *Magna Graecia* eft appellata quia a *Tarento* ufque ad *Cumas* omnes *Chalcidici Graeci* condiderunt.

FESTUS, not more fatisfactorily,

Major Graecia dicta eft *Italia* quod cam Siculi quondam obtinuerunt, vel quod in eâ multae magnaeque civitates fuerunt ex *Graecia* profectae. PYTHAGORAS's Panegyrifts from to align better Reafons, one of whom, JAMBLICHUS, expreßly affirms that this Title was owing to the Splendour and Fame it acquired from the Difcipline and Doctrines of that extraordinary Man, and the early excellent Scholars formed by him. Ἀπὸ δὲ Τούτων τῶν καταλογαίων ἐκεῖνα το̃ Ἰταλίας πᾶσαι φιλοσόφων ἀνδρῶν μεϛαλύνετο, καὶ πρότερον ἀγνοουμένη μετὰ δηγ⟨…⟩ δε ΠυΘαγοραϛ Μεγάλη ΕΛΛΑΔα ελλήνων, εἰ ώδεινε τᾶϛ ὀλῆϛ ωὐδε φιλοσόφοϛ εἰ Πλεῖσται· ὠ Κροτωνίαϛ γινο̃ϛαν C. 29. And well might that Country (fays SYNESIUS) be called *Magna Graecia*, where PYTHAGORAS's Scholars became Governors of States; where CHARONDAS and ZALEUCUS gave Laws; where ARCHYTAS and PHILOLAUS commanded Armies; and TIMÆUS, the Prince of Aftronomers,

was employed in Embaffies and in other Departments of civil Adminiftration. —— Where fuch Men as thefe were Minifters and Statefmen, need we wonder that *Italy* flourifhed fo well, even to the ninth Generation after PYTHAGORAS? P. 308.

Πολλὰ μὲν γὰρ καὶναὶ τας ἄλλαϛ ἡσκεῖ Παιδεύματα καντεϛ αἱ τῶν πόλεων ἀρχαὶ, ΧΑΛΚΙ ὁ ΧΑΡΩΝΔΑϛ πρωτηγορὼ, ἔι φάίν τὸ δὴγ κατὶ ἰγ ΧΑΛΚΙΔΙ με καθ᾽ ἡμᾶϛ εἰϛ ΖΑΛΕΥΚΟϛ, στρατηγοὶ δὲ ἀρχύταϛ, καὶ Φιλόλαοϛ, ἳ δὴ προϛαγορεύεϛ Τίμαιοϛ ἀϛρονόμοϛ ὁ καὶ σοφίαϛ προελθὼν εἰϛ ἄκρα, τοσοῦδε ἐπήνεγκε το̃ Πόλεων διετηρεῖτο. ΣΥΝΕΣΙϛ Ορ. Fc. P. 308.

(2) Metapontini cum *Sybaritis* & *Crotoniatibus* pellere cæteros *Graeci Italia* Statuerunt.

JUSTIN XX. 2.

(3) It fhould feem, that after the *Romans* had obliterated the Name of *G R Æ C I A*, they were ftill willing to preferve the *M A G N A*; at leaft VIRGIL is particularly fond of applying it to *Italy*,

Seu vos HESPERIAM MAGNAM Saturniaque Arva,
Æn. I. 573.

Sed nunc ITALIAM MAGNAM Grynæus APOLLO.
IV. 345.

Multi illum MAGNO e LATIO totaque petebant *Aufonia*. ——
VII. 54.

(4) Notum eft *Pæftum* a *Dorenfibus* conftitutum, C. VIII. 2.

(5) *Mazochii* Commentaria in ÆNEAS Tabulas *Heraclenfes*. fo. *Neapoli*, 1754.

early as any other Wanderers after the Difperfion. His principal Argument depends on tracing the two Names, *Pæftum* and *Pofidonia*, to the fame Radix in the *Oriental* Languages.

ACCORDING to BOCHART, (1) the *Heathen* Traditions concerning SATURN and his three Sons, agree well with the facred Hiftory of NOAH and his Sons; particularly that Prophecy relative to the Fate of JAPHET and his Pofterity; *God fhall enlarge* JAPHET (2). By *whofe Sons*, we are told afterwards, *that the Ifles of the* Gentiles *were divided in their Lands.* Thefe Circumftances very exactly correfpond with the Hiftory of NEPTUNE and his Children, of whom LACTANTIUS mentions, from the ancient Hiftorian EUHEMERUS, that JUPITER *gave him the Government of the Sea, its Iflands, and all maritime Coafts* (3). As to the Meaning of the Word ΠΟΣΕΙΔΩΝ we fhall in vain, according to HERODOTUS, (4) look for it among the *Greeks*, to whom the *Lybians* furnifhed this Deity and his Name. But in the *Oriental* Dialects is to be found פשטן *Pefitan*, fignifying *wide* or *extended*; and as it is well known how frequent the Changes are between the T and the D, by admitting of the Change in this Word we fhall have one very like to Ποσειδαν in. the *Doric* Dialect, which comes the nearest of all the Dialects to thofe of the *Orientalt* (5). Now it is remarkable enough, that the Word ΠΑΙΣΤΑΝΟ, found on the Medals No. 41 and 42, on one Side of which is the Head of NEPTUNE, and on the other his Son TARENS on a Dolphin, fhould fo nearly correfpond with BOCHART's Derivation of the Word ΠΟΣΕΙΔΑΝ, who does not feem to have been much beholden to Medals for any Affiftances in his learned Enquiries, though undoubtedly he might have received much from them (6).

IF this Etymology of the Name *Pæftum* be admitted, it will follow, that it was prior to *Pofidonia*, fubftituted in its Room by fome *Grecian* Colonifts, who fucceeded the original Inhabitants; many Inftances may be produced of the *Greeks* either foftening the Termination of the old Names of Places which they took Poffeffion of, or elfe fubftituting others of the fame Meaning in their own Language.

THE oldeft Author that gives any Account of *Greeks* fettling here, is the Geographer SCYMNUS CHIUS, who flourifhed about ninety Years before CHRIST, and who, defcribing the Inhabitants of *Italy*, fays, " Next to thefe are the *Oenotrians*, extending as far as " *Pofidonia*, where, they fay, the *Sybarites* formerly brought a Colony (7)." This is confirmed by STRABO, who writes thus: " Next to the *Campanians* and *Samnites* are " the *Picentins*, brought by the *Romans* to the *Pofidonian* Bay, now called the *Pæftan*, " as the City *Pofidonia* is called *Pæftum*, which lies in the Middle of the Bay. The

---

(1) *Phalg.* I. 1.

Gen. X. 27. ומי אשים שם (2)

(3) JUPITER imperium NEPTUNO dat maris, et infulis omnibus & quæ finibus maris loca funt omnibus regionem.
De foffa religione. I. 11.

(4) *Euterp.* 30.

(5) BOCHART *Phalg.* I. 1.

(6) MASOCHIUS, P. 500.

(7) Πρωτοι δε τωδε των πολυ Οινωπαι Μερα την Ποσειδωνα ωνομασμενη Ην φασι Συβαριται αντωσαν εστι.

V. 243.

" *Sybarites*

" *Sybarites* built a Wall to the Sea, obliging the Inhabitants to retire farther up into
" the Country (1)."

FROM STRABO's Account we may gather, that the *Sybarites* found a Town already
built, which they firft furrounded with a Wall; and, therefore, whatever Splendour and
Magnificence it had to boaft of, was probably pofterior to the Arrival of the *Sybarites,*
and wholly owing to them. Whatever Inhabitants were then found there, whether
Dorians from *Phœnicia* or from *Greece*, or whether the old *Oenotrians*, mentioned by
STRABO (2), it is not to be fuppofed, that if they had had Riches and Tafte enough to
have erected fuch magnificent Buildings as thofe whofe Remains are here exhibited, that
they would have left them naked and expofed to every hoftile Invader; and yet this
Opinion feems to have been adopted by fome late Writers (3).

THE Hiftory then of the *Sybarites* may be confidered alfo, in fome Meafure, as that
of the *Pofidonians*; and, therefore, we fhall prefent our Readers with fome Traits of
their Characters, as they lie difperfed in different ancient Authors.

SYBARIS, lying at the upper End of the Gulph of *Tarentum*, was firft fettled by a
joint Colony of *Acheans* and *Trœzenians* (4), who, not agreeing long together in their
new Settlement, the latter were expelled thence by the former (5). Thefe, by Degrees,
grew to fuch Extent of Power and Territory, as to be one of the moft confiderable
States of *Magna Græcia*; they had the Command over four neighbouring States and
twenty-five Cities, and were able at one Time to bring 300000 Men into the Field
againft their Enemies and Neighbours the *Crotonians*. Of their intermediate Hiftory,
from their Foundation to this Period, which did not long precede their utter Deftruction,
we know little more than fome very extraordinary Defcriptions of their Luxury, fcattered
in ancient Writers. They laid it down as a Maxim, that he who would not die an
untimely Death, fhould never get up from Table, nor out of his Bed, to fee the Rays
of the fetting or the rifing Sun. They excufed their Fifhermen from all Taxes and
Impofitions; they publifhed honorary Rewards for thofe who exhibited the moft fumptuous
Entertainments, or invented a new Difh. Notice was given a very confiderable length

(1) Μᾶλλὸν δὲ τὰς Καμπανοὺς· καὶ τὰ Σαγαιὰ —— τὰ τᾶς Πλαμίνας νᾶας τοῦτ
—— τὰτῳ Πομπαίου περνωπμρᾶτος τᾶς τᾶς Πιτσηλωποτᾶς σηλαῳ, ἦ τᾶς Παραᾶτῶ
σαλολᾶαι, ὡς ἡ πάλιᾳ ἢ Πᾶσυϊλωσα, Παῦτις, τᾶ μαῶγ τῳ σσλῳ ὁπρος. Σκηγῳῶω
μᾶτ ὁτ τᾶτ δαλαττῳ τοιγᾶτ ὁἰλᾶ, ὁ Υ ομᾶφϊλᾶτ ναᾶφρα μετατᾶται. STRABO, 251.

(2) Πρως ὁὲ τᾶτ Ἐλλᾶνᾳᾳ ὄλλων, οὐ ὐσαᾳ ᾳτ Ἀνᾱᾳᾳαῳ Κιῶηᾳ ἡ ᾳ Οικηᾳᾳᾳ
τᾶτ τᾱθτᾳ τᾱμαθᾱᾳ. Ibid. 253.

(3) Par le gout & par les proportions de ces Edifices, par leur
refemblance avec ceux qui fubfiftent encore dans la baute *Egypte*, il eft
aifé de fe convaincre que leur Conftruction a procedé la Naiffance
des Arts meme chez les *Grecs*.
  Obfervations fur l'Italie par deux Gentilhommes *Sardoifes*,
  T. II. p. 244.

(4) ARIST. *Polit.* L. V. C. 3.

(5) If one was to indulge a Conjecture concerning the firft
Greeks that fettled at *Pofidonia*, it fhould be, that thefe *Trœzenians*

thus expelled, wandered to the *Pofidonian* Bay, and there took
Poffeffion of that Village, which they furrounded with a Wall,
and gave it the Name of the Metropolis which they once inhabited
in *Old Greece*. For STRABO informs us, that *Trœze* was formerly
called *Pofidonia*, 373. The Inhabitants having a particular Veneration
for NEPTUNE, into which they were compelled, as PAUSANIUS
relates, II. 32. by that Deity's fpoiling all their Fruits with
Showers of Salt; till his Anger was appeafed by their erecting
and dedicating a Temple NEPTUNO σωτῆρι. Here was THESEUS
born, called thence by OVID the *Neptunian Hero*,
  His tecum Trœzena colam Pittheïa regna,
      Jam nunc eft Patria Grenïor illa mea:
  Temper abeft, aberitque diu Neptunius Heros
      Illum Pirithei detinet ora fui.
                          Ep. IV. 107.
Let it be obferved alfo on PAUSANIUS's Authority, that, after
the Return of the *Heraclidœ* into *Peloponnefus*, the *Trœzenians* admitted
fome *Dorians* to fettle amongft them.

T

of

of Time before-hand, of thefe Entertainments, that the Ladies might have Time to
furnifh themfelves with proper Dreffes for the Occafion. A *Sybarite*, invited to an
Entertainment at *Lacedæmon*, was fo difgufted at the Coarfenefs of his Fare, that he faid,
he wondered not the *Spartans* made fuch good Soldiers, for that Death was preferable
to fuch Living (1).

Thus enervated, they quarrelled with their Neighbours the *Crotonians*, againft whom
they took the Field with 300000 Men, and were entirely defeated. A dreadful Carnage
enfued, for the Victors fpared none that did not fave themfelves by Flight, and deftroyed
the devoted City, by turning the River through it (2).

Those who had efcaped, returned in a little Time afterwards to their defolated City,
which they did not long enjoy, being again expelled by the *Crotonians*. They then
applied to their Mother Country, *Attica*, for Affiftance, who fent a Fleet with new
Settlers; which, neglecting the Old City, founded another at a little Diftance, to which
they gave the Name of *Thurium* (3): But the reftlefs Spirit of the *Sybarites* being very
troublefome to their new Allies, they experienced the fame Ufage from them, which
they themfelves had formerly dealt to the *Trœzenians*, and were, for the laft Time,
forever expelled from their old Habitations (4).

The Time and Occafion of this fatal Conteft with the *Crotonians* are pretty diftinctly
marked by Diodorus Siculus.

There was a Demagogue at *Sybaris*, who prevailed on the People to banifh five
Hundred of the richeft Citizens, and to confifcate their Eftates. The Exiles fled for
Refuge to *Crotona*, whither Ambaffadors were fent from *Sybaris* to require their being
delivered up, and in Cafe of Refufal to denounce War: A Council being called to
deliberate on the Affair, the *Crotonians*, fearful of contending with a fuperior Power,

---

(1) Athenæus. L. XII. P. 518. Plinius. L. III. C. 11.
Plutarch in *Conviv:* 7. *Sapient.* Senec. *de ira*, XII.
There are many Proverbs extant referring to the luxurious Manners
of the *Sybarites*.
Συςαρίων τρυτη Sybaritica Menfa.
Συςαριαι πχγται Sybaritica Solutiones. Max. Tyr. III.
Sybaritici Libelli. Martial.
Sybariticus miffus. Lampridius.

(2) Diod. Sic. XII. 234.

(3) The future Seat of this new Colony we fhall give from
Strabo. It flourifhed much, for a confiderable Time, under
the aufpicious Influence of Charondas's Laws, till it was
reduced to Slavery by the *Lucanians*; who, in their Turn, being
oppreffed by the *Tarentines*, applied to the *Romans* for Protection,
and they fent a Colony hither, A. U. C. 560, and called the
City *Copia*.

(4) Where fome of them, thus expelled, fled for Refuge, we
are told by Herodotus in a remarkable Paffage. Diodorus &
ταῦτα διαπονησάντες τῶν Βαρβάρων, οἱ ἐκπίπτοντες ἐκ βοηθείας το
ανθρωπων τῶν κοινῶν, καὶ τῶν ἐκπίπτεσθαι ... [illegible]

Μαυραίων ὄντων ἡ δε φιλονεικία τῶν ἀρχαίων, οἱ τοιοῦς ῥητοι ἀρχειν..... Πλειε
γαρ ... [illegible] ... ἀπῳκησαν.
"The *Athenians*, driven from their Habitations by the *Perfians*,
"the Sybarites, who, after their Expulfion, went to
"inhabit the Cities of Laos and Scidrus, requifited not
"to the *Miffians* the Civilities they had received from them;
"for, after the *Croanians* had taken *Sybaris*, all the *Athenians*, arrived
"to *Pofhorny*, fhewed their Heads, and gave public Demonftrations
"of their Sorrow. Thefe two Cities had been more ftrongly
"united in Friendfhip than any I ever knew." VL. 21.
And no Wonder, when thefe two fuch a Sympathy of Manners
between them, the *Athenians* being as remarkable for their Luxury
as the *Sybarites*. Their *Athenian* Wool, and the Cloths made of it,
furnifhed out the richeft and moft extravagant Dreffes, and no
Doubt, made a Part of the Finery, not only of the *Sybarites*, but
of the other *Italian Greeks*; yet, Dr. Bentley brings this as one
Argument to prove the *Spurioufnefs* of Xaleucus's Laws, that
among other luxurious Articles, the wearing *Milefian* Cloths fhould
be forbidden to the *Locrians*; by whom, fays he, confidering their
Remotenefs from *Afia*, it is not likely they could ever have
been fo much as heard of. *Diff. on Phalaris*, P. 350.

§ Athenæus, P. 519.

were much inclined to fubmit to the Demand; till PYTHAGORAS efpoufing the Caufe of the Exiles, prevailed on the *Crotoniani* to fupport them.

Now PYTHAGORAS came into *Italy* in the Time of TARQUINIUS SUPERBUS, where, as CICERO informs us (1), he taught in *Magna Græcia* with the greateft Reputation, Authority and Succefs; this was about the fixty-fecond Olympiad, or the two hundredth and twentieth Year of *Rome*, and about the five hundredth and twentieth Year before the Birth of CHRIST; foon after which we may date the fatal Overthrow of the *Sybarites* by the *Crotoniani*.

IT is probable that, about this Time, a Colony of them took poffeffion of *Pofidonia*, and we need not doubt imported thither all the Refinements of Art from their native City. Here they feem to have continued in Eafe and Profperity for near two hundred Years; during which Period, we may fuppofe thofe noble Buildings, whofe Remains are here exhibited, were conftructed. This Period may indeed be called the Golden Age of *Magna Græcia*, all owing to the Difcipline, Laws and Example of PYTHAGORAS and his Scholars, of which he had a confiderable Number from every State, *Barbarian* as well as *Greek*; and who being engaged in the Adminiftration of the Affairs of their refpective Countries, exhibited fuch beautiful Models of Government, as were not at that Time to be parallelled any where elfe: In particular they are celebrated for religioufly keeping the Laws themfelves, and abftaining from the public Treafure (2).

WHAT a Pity but that fome one of them had given us a Hiftory of this happy Æra, to which none of the old *Greek* or *Roman* Hiftorians feem to have been able or willing to do juftice? TULLY indeed acknowledges in general, that *Rome* muft have been beholden to PYTHAGORAS and his Difciples for many Improvements: But he excufes himfelf from pointing them out in particular, for which, like a true *Roman*, he gives this Reafon; " Left we fhould feem to have borrowed from others what are fuppofed " to be the Effects of our own Genius (3)." LIVY is quite indignant at the Suppofition, that NUMA could have been beholden to PYTHAGORAS for any Part of his Knowledge or Difcipline (4); and when in the three hundredth Year of *Rome*, a Decemvirate was

---

(1) PYTHAGORAS, qui cum regnante TARQUINIO SUPERBO in *Italiam* veniffet, tenuit *Magnam illam Graciam* cum honore & difciplina tum etiam Auctoritate. *Tufc. Quæft.* I. 16. and IV. 1. But the fineft Picture of his Succefs there may be feen in JUSTIN, who fays,

Crotonam venit, populumque in luxuriam lapfam, auctoritate fua ad ufum frugalitatis revocavit. Laudabat quotidie virtutem, vitia luxuriæ, cafufque civitatum ea pefte perditarum enumerabat, tantumque ftudium ad frugalitatem multitudinis provocavit ut aliquos ex his luxuriatos incredibile videretur.

Matronarum quoque feparatim a viris doctrinam & puerorum a parentibus frequenter habuit. Docebat nunc has pudicitiam & obfuqula in viros, nunc illos modeftiam & literarum ftudium. Inter hæc, velut genticiæm virtutum, frugalitatem omnibus ingerebat. Lib. XX. 4.

(2) Και γαρ ηρας, εβασιλευε οι ταδιτα Ιταλιας λεγεται των — συγχαιοι η ηγεισαι πραττει — ει ταην δε τη ηγμην βασιλεια καλουπαι τον Ποσδιων ... Πόλιν γεγοεβαι ω εν Ιταλια. Ipfi legis obfervabant & Iudices urbes rexerunt abftinentes a publicis reditibus. Eo tempore pulcherrima refpublicæ & in *Italia* & in *Sicilia* videntur exftitiffe.

JAMBLICHUS, 119.

(3) Quis eft enim qui putet, cum faveret in *Italia* GRÆCIA potentiffima & maxima urbibus ea quæ MAGNA dicta eft, in hifque primum ipfius PYTHAGORÆ deinde poftea PYTHAGOREORUM tantum nomen effet, noftrorum hominum ad eorum doctriffimas voces aures claufas fuiffe? ——

Multa etiam funt in noftris inftituatis, ducta ab illa, quæ prætereo ne ea, quæ peperiffe ipfi putamur, aliunde didiciffe videamur. *Tufc. Quæft.* IV. 1.

(4) Euopte igitur ingenio temperatum animum virtutibus fuiffe opinor magis, la ftructaeque non tam peregrinis artibus, quam difciplina tetrica ac trifti veterum Sabinorum.

LIV. 1. 18.

appointed

appointed for the compiling a Code of Laws, and proper Perſons choſen to travel and examine thoſe of other Nations, LIVY only ſpecifies old *Greece* (1), whilſt DION. HALICARNASSENSIS, giving an Account of ROMULUS's Speech on this Oecaſion, ſays, that he propoſed ſending theſe Ambaſſadors not only to old *Greece*, but likewiſe to the Cities of *Magna Græcia*, to which Propoſition, he adds, the Senate aſſented (2). And conſidering the Reputation of the Laws of thoſe States, drawn up by ZALEUCUS, CHARONDAS, and others, this Account is highly probable ; for in the little Portions of their Hiſtory, given us by STRABO and others, their being governed by good Laws (3), generally makes a Part of the Panegyric, and this not only with regard to the *Locrians* and the *Thurians*, but the ſame is ſaid of *Valia* (4), the Birth-Place of ZENO and PARMENIDES, *Pythagoreans* ; ſituated at a very little Diſtance, and in the ſame Bay with *Poſidonia*.

THE happy Repoſe which theſe States, thus well adminiſtered, long enjoyed, was about the Year of *Rome* 360, diſturbed by the Hero of thoſe Times, DIONYSIUS, the famous Tyrant of *Sicily*, who having driven the *Carthaginians* from that Iſland, reſolved to fall upon his Neighbours the *Italian Greeks*: It does not appear indeed that they had ever offended him, but yet the Reaſons produced by the Hiſtorian for his attacking them, are probably as good as any of thoſe that have been alledged by the Heroes of any Times for an offenſive War (5). Accordingly, he lands in *Italy*, and making an Alliance with the *Lucanians*, gains repeated Victories over the *Græcian* States, which had united all their Forces, and formed a Confederacy among themſelves to oppoſe the common Enemy (6) ; but DIONYSIUS was called back to *Sicily* before he had time to improve his Victories, and left the *Greeks* thus weakened, to cope with much more formidable and obſtinate Enemies. Theſe were the old *Aborigines* of the Country, who, jealous of the growing Power of the *Romans* on the one hand, and the *Greeks* on the other, reſolved to unite in making an Effort to preſerve their Liberties and Properties. Accordingly, about the Year of *Rome*, 413, the *Samnites* began that famous War with the *Romans*, which laſted, with various Turns of Fortune, above ſeventy Years.

---

(1) Miſſi legati *Athenas* juſſique inclytas leges Solonis deſcribere & aliarum civitatum Inſtituta mores juraque noſcere.

LIV. III. 31.

(2) Πρεσβεις ἐστελλεν, τας μεν εις τας Ελλαδας πολεις τας ἐν Ιταλῃ, Τας δε εις Αθηνας αιτησομενος παρα των Ελληνων τας νομους τας κρατιστας τρμας καὶ μαθησομενας τας διαθεσεις σφετεριζεσθαι ὅσας τινων δεῃ. Legati electi, quorum alii ad *Græcas* civitates in *Italia*, alii ad *Athenas* miſſi, leges optimas & noſtris moribus maxime accommodatas huc transferrent.

DION. HAL. X. 51.

(3) Πασαν χρονον ωμολεγειας. Longo tempore optimis legibus uteretur.

STRABO, 259.

(4) Εἰ οἱ Παρμενιδης και Ζηνων εγενετο Αιλης Πυθαγορικοι, δοκει δε μοι καὶ ἡ πολις αυτη δι ανδρας τουτους. Ex qua PARMENIDES & ZENO, PYTHAGORÆ diſcipuli, per illos atque etiam antea videtur mihi bene adminiſtrata fuiſſe.

Ibid. Agr.

(5) DIONYSIUS, e Sicilia *Carthaginienſibus* pulſis, occupatoque totius inſulæ imperio, grave otium regno ſuo, periculoſumque

deſidiam rati, exercitum ratus, copias in Italiam trajecit, ſimul ut militum viris conſuetos labore neutiquam & reguli fines proferrentur. Prima noſtras advectis Græcis qui proximis Italiri maris litera conſiſtat, fuit ; quibus devictis, ſtolidos quoſque aggreditur, omneſque Graeci nominis *Italiae* poſſidentis hostes ſibi deſtinat ; quæ gentes non partem ſed univerſam finium ſtatum ea tempeſtate occupaverunt.

JUSTIN. XX. 1.

(6) Ὁ δε τω Ιταλιαν καθοικος *Αλληνες* πρας μεν μεγα των εαυτων χρησε προεσαντος των *Αμωνιων* ὑβρισθεις, συμπιπτον ἡ απι αλληλας τεμνονται, οι εντιθει τρυσαλτυνεσθε. σπευδα γαρ τω ευταρ σαλον εμπεσθαι, οι τας γωγωσας Αιγνων αισελζεῖν, οι τρις δια της Σικιλιας πρας αυτη *Graeci* qui incolebant *Italiam* videntes DIONYSII avaritiam rerum regionas inhientem, ſocietatem inter ſe & communem concilio locum conſtituebant, ita facilius Sperabant ſeſe contra DIONYSIUM ſe defendere, tuto etiam contra *Lucanos*, qui contra illos eodem tempore bellum gerebant.

DIOD. SIC. XIV. 9.

About the fame Time, the *Brettians* and the *Lucanians* attacked the *Græcian* States; *Pofidonia* foon fell a Prey to the latter (1), who in confequence, as it fhould feem, of a general Plan for eftablifhing the Superiority they fhould acquire on a lafting Foundation, not only changed its Name to *Pæftum* (2), but endeavoured to alter, as fpeedily and as effectually as they could, the Language, Manners and Cuftoms of its Inhabitants. Of thefe Circumftances we have a very affecting Defcription in Athenæus, who produces this remarkable Paffage out of Aristoxenus, a celebrated Mufician and Philofopher of *Tarentum* (3). " We are doing, *fays he*, much the fame, as the *Pofidonians* on the *Tyrrhene* " Bay, who, being originally *Greeks*, are now barbarized, being become *Tyrrhenes*, or rather " *Romans*; thefe meeting together on one of their old Feftivals, recalled to memory their " ancient Names and Cuftoms, for the Lofs of which they indulged a focial Grief, and " parted in Tears; fo we, now that our Theatres are become barbarous, and the general " Tafte in Mufic fo corrupted, meet together, a flender Party, to lament the Change, and " recollect what Mufic once was (4)." Thefe were indeed hard Conditions impofed by the *Barbarians* on this, as well as on the other polite States of *Magna Græcia*; infomuch, that when Hanno wanted to introduce a Colony of *Brettians* into *Crotona*, the Inhabitants declared that they would fooner die, than by fuch a Mixture give up their ancient Laws, Cuftoms and Language (5). However, this came to be the general Fortune of the *Greek* States in no long Space of Time: But to divert the evil Day as long as they could, they called in Alexander, King of *Epirus*, to their Affiftance: He was Brother to Olympias, the Mother of Alexander the Great, who was meditating the Conqueft of the Eaft, whilft his Uncle flattered himfelf with the hopes of as plentiful a Harveft of Laurels in the Weft: And in this Fortune feemed at firft to confirm thofe Hopes; for making a Defcent at *Pæftum*, he attacked and routed the combined Forces of the *Samnites* and the *Lucanians* near it (6). This was in the Year of *Rome* 418. Flufhed with this Succefs, he continued the War for fome Years; and, in a Series of Invafions which he made from *Epirus*, took many of the Cities belonging to the *Lucanians* and the *Brettians*; but found, at laft, that he had to deal with Adverfaries of a very different Character from thofe over which he heard that his Nephew of *Macedonia* had triumphed

(1) Ἅμα δὲ καὶ τοῖ Ἕλλωσι ναὶ ναδξιδοῖ τιαχαλῶσι μιχρι πάχρωσ τάςχιʼσα, πολὺσ χρόσοσ πυσυλιμᾶι δε ἢ Ἕλλαρεσ αῖ ὁι Βαρβαστοι πυχε ἀδλάλοισ.

Simul etiam *Graci* utrumque litus ufque ad fretum tenuerunt; diu inter fe *Barbari* & *Graci* certaverunt.

                  Strabo, 255.

Οἱ δὲ Ἀσσανοὶ —— Πωσιδωνιάται δε και τοὺς Συρμάχαις ἐμίσωσάισ πόλοσρ, καὶʼηχε ταῖς πολιχ πισιω.

Lucani — fuperatis bello *Pofidoniatis* atque eorum fociis Urbes illorum obtinuerunt.

                  Ibid. 254.

(2) Poffibly reftored its original Name. After this Period we find it called by this Name in Livy and other *Latin* Writers.

(3) Aristoxenus muficus vir, literarum veterum diligentiffimus, Aristotelis philofophi auditor. A. Gellius. IV. 11.

Aristoxenus was a Scholar of Aristotle, and expected to have fucceeded his Mafter in his School; but finding Theophrastus preferred to him, he amufed himfelf with the reft of his Life with making and writing mifcellaneous Collections. Theophrastus fucceeded Aristotle in his School about the Year of *Rome* 425. So that probably Aristoxenus wrote this not many Years after

Pofidonia's being in Poffeffion of the *Lucanians*, and long before it was a *Roman* Colony, which was in the Year of *Rome* 480.

(4) Ὅμοιον φαμι ποιησαι Πωσιδωνιάταις τοῖς ἐν τῷ Τυρρηνικῷ κόλπῳ κατοικοσσιν, οἷς πάλιτα, τε μὲν εξ ἀρχῆς Ἕλλασω σοσι, κεʼνιναβαρβαρῶσοι, Τυρρηνοις ἢ Ῥωμαίοις γεγονόσι, καὶ τεν τε φωνὴν μεθαβεβλησεσαι, ναʼν λοιπὰ τῶν ἐπιτηδευμάτων· ἀγοισι τε μαν τῶν εορτῶν ἔτι μίαν τῶν Ἑλληνικῶν ἢ και σον, ἦ ἢ ποικιλῶν συναγόμενοιολι τῶν ἀρχαίων ὀνόματων ὑπομιμνήσκονται και τῶν σπιμων. ἀναθρηνησαντες δὲ πρός ἀλλήλοις και ἀποδακρύσαντες ἀπέρχονται. ἰδε δε οι φασι και ἡμεῖς ποιδ και ʼλα δικτρα σεβαρβάρωσαι, και εἰς μεγάλην διαφθοραν προεληλυθεν ἢ πανδημος αὐτη μουσικη, καθʼ αὐτοι γενόμενοι ολίγοι αναμιμνῆσκομε εμαυθα ἱα τι ἢ μουσικη.

                  XII. 7.

(5) Morituros fe affirmabant citius quam inmixti Bruttiis in alienos ritus, mores, legefque ac mox linguam etiam verterentur.

                  Liv. XXIV. 3.

(6) *Samnites* bellum Alexandri Epirenfi in *Lucanos* traxit, qui duo populi adverfus regem extenfionem a *Pæfto* (lege, ad *Pæftum*) facientem fignis conlatis pugnaverunt; eo certamine fuperior Alexander.

                  Ibid. VIII. 17.

in the East; which he expressed, by saying, " that he had attacked a Country inhabited
" by Men, and his Nephew one by Women (1)." He was at length defeated and slain in
an Engagement with the *Lucanians*, who, with their Confederates the *Samnites*, being
sufficiently weakened in their long Contests with foreign and domestic Enemies, were
forced at last to submit to the *Romans*. This Event entirely changed the face of Affairs
in *Italy*.

THE *Græcian* States now grew jealous of the encreasing Power of the *Romans*, to
check which, they invited PYRRHUS, King of *Epirus*, to their Assistance. He was the
first Foreigner that had waged War with the *Romans*, against whom, in conjunction with
the *Greeks* and *Barbarians*, he carried it on with great Vigour for six Years, but was
entirely defeated in the Year of *Rome* 478. This Defeat furnished a very singular
Triumph to the Conquerors; the Elephants which he had brought into *Italy*, and which
the *Romans* called *Lucanian* Oxen, the rich Ornaments of the *Greek* Cities, and the
Captives of the different Nations of the *Epirots, Thessalians, Macedonians, Brettians,
Lucanians, Samnites* and *Tarentines*, all exhibited a more magnificent Spectacle to the
Romans than they had ever yet been gratified with. The Consequence of this Defeat
and Triumph, was the almost entire Reduction of the several States of *Italy* to the *Roman*
Power; and their Cities being either made Municipal Towns, or forced to admit of
Roman Colonies. Accordingly we find, from the Epitome to LIVY's fourteenth Book,
that a Colony was sent to *Posidonia*, which VELLEIUS PATERCULUS also mentions, and
fixes the Time to the Year of *Rome* 481 (2).

THE next Mention in History made of *Pæstum*, is not till fifty-six Years afterward;
when, after the Defeat of the *Romans* by HANNIBAL at the Battle of *Thrasymene*, they
sent their golden Cups, a free Gift, to *Rome* (3); but the haughty Spirit of the *Romans*
was not yet sunk low enough to accept of this Relief from their Colonists; to whom,
however, the fatal Battle of *Cannæ* soon afterwards reduced them to the Necessity of
applying for Supplies both of Men and Money; and then they had the Mortification to
be refused by eighteen Colonies out of thirty: Among those, whose Names are
mentioned, as faithful to their Engagements, we find the *Pæstans*. " By the Assistance
" of these Colonies, *says the Historian*, (4), was the *Roman* Empire supported in its greatest

---

(1) Sic quidem ad *Romanos* ire quasi in *adscitos, Macedonem* illi
ad *Persas* quasi in *Eventibus.*

A. GELLIUS, XVII. 21.

A. GELLIUS says ad *Romanos*; but JUSTIN tells us, that
ALEXANDER had made a League with them, L. VIII. and very
probably; for the *Lucaniani* and *Samnites* were then common Enemies
to them both. The same Mistake is made by ATHENÆUS in the
Quotation on the foregoing Page, where the *Tyrrheni*; or *Romans*
are put for the *Lucanians.*

(2) Coloniæ deductæ sunt *Pysdonia* & *Cossa.* LIV. Epit. XIV.
Ad *Cossam* & *Pæstum* annos firme trecentos FABIO DORSONE
& C. CANINO Coss. Colmi missi.   VELL. PAT. I. 13.
Iisdem consulibus coloniæ deductæ sunt *Cossa* in *Volscientibus* &
in *Lucania Pæstum* quæ Græcis *Posidonia* vocatur.   EADEM EODEM.

Sybaritis domerant, ab his recens in ditionem populi *Romani*
pervenerat.   *Frinstenii Supplem.* in LIV. XIV.

(3) Legati a *Pæste* pateras aureas *Romam* attulerunt, iis sicut
Neapolitanii gratiæ actæ, aurum non acceptum.

LIVIUS. XXII. 36.

(4) Ne nunc quidem post tot sæcula sileantur fraudenturve
laude sui — ab altero mari *Pæniani* & PÆSTANI & *Cossani*
— Harum coloniarum subsidio tum imperium populi *Romani* stetit,
Iisque gratiæ & in senatu & apud populum actæ. Duodecim
aliarum coloniarum quæ detrectaverant imperium, mentionem fieri
natios voluerunt, neque illos demiri, neque retineri, neque appellari
a consulibus. Ea tacita castigatio maxime ex dignitate populi
Romani visa est.

LIVIUS. XXVII. 10.

" Extremity;

" Extremity; Thanks were returned to them from the Senate and the People, and their
" Names ordered to be recorded with Honour.   Of those who refused, the Senate
" resolved that no notice should be taken; such silent Contempt being most agreeable
" to the Majesty of the *Roman* People."   On this Occasion, probably, the golden
Cups of *Pæstum* were accepted, and made Part of the great Heap of Gold then
collected (1).   About the same Time they assisted the *Romans* with Ships according to
Treaty, which made part of the Fleet that sailed under the Command of D. QUINTIUS
to relieve *Tarentum* (2).

FROM this Time we hear no more of *Pæstum*, till we come to the Poets of the
Augustan Age, and their Successors, who agree in celebrating the fine Roses which it
produced in great Abundance, and their blossoming twice a Year (3).

NOTWITHSTANDING this happy Temperature of the Soil and Climate, STRABO tells
us, that in his Time the Country was unwholesome, on account of the River having
broke its Channel, and stagnating in Marshes round it (4).

THUS much for the ancient State of *Pæstum* to the Time of AUGUSTUS: For its
History from that Time to the present, our Materials grow still more scanty; as we find
no mention made of it in Writers till the Invasion of *Italy* by the *Saracens*, who, after
conquering *Africa* and *Spain*, got Possession of *Sicily* about the Year of Christ 820;
from whence, about twenty Years afterwards, they took an Opportunity of some civil
Commotions between the States of *Italy* to pass over thither ; where, after committing
horrid Devastations, they settled themselves at *Agropoli*, in the Neighbourhood of
Pæstum (5).

HERE they became powerful and formidable ; insomuch, that DOCIBILIS, Duke of
Gaeta, courted their Assistance against PANDENULF Count of *Capua*, who had got a

(1) Prompta ad quatuor millia pondo auri.
                                LIV. XXVII. 10.

(2) Postremo ipse a Sociis, Rheginisque & a Velia, & a *Pæsto*
debitas ex foedere exigendo, classem viginti navium, sicut ante
dictum est, effecit.
                                Ibid XXVI. 39.

(3) Forsitan & pingues hortos quæ cura colendi
Ornaret, canerem, biferique rosaria *Pæsti*.
                                VIRG. Geo. IV. 118.
Leucosiamque petit, tepidique rosaria *Pæsti*.
                                OVID. Met. XV. 708.
Nec *Babylon* æstum, nec frigora Pontus habebit,
Callidaque *Posthumus* vincet odore rosas,
Quam ibi nostrarum veniet oblivio rerum,
Nam ita pars fati candida nulla mei.
                                Ex Ponto 11, 4, 27.
Vidi ego odorati victura rosaria *Pæsti*
Sub matutino coctà jacere noto.
                                PROPERTIUS IV. 5, 59.
Pæstanis rubeant æmula labra rosis.
                                MARTIAL IV. 42, 10.
Fragravit art quod rosarium *Pæsti*.
                                Ib. V. 38, 9.

Tantaque *Pæstani* gloria ruris erat.
                                Ib. VI. 80. 6.
Speaking of a Garland of Roses, he says,
Seu Tu *Pæstanis* genita es, seu Tiburis arvis,
Seu rubuit tellus Tusculæ flore tuo.
                                Ib. IX. 61.
Prataque nec hibero cessura rosaria *Pæsto*,
Quodque viret Jani Mense, nec alget olus.
                                Ib. XII. 31.
Pæstana violas, & cana ligustra columa,
Hyblæis apibus *Corsica* mella dabit.
                                Ib. I. 9, 27.
Vidi *Pæstano* gaudere rosaria cultu
Exoriente novo roscida Lucifero.
                                AUSONIUS, Id. XIV.
Adsurgit ceu forte minor sub matre virente
Laurus, & ingentes ramos, olimque futuras
Promittit jam parva comas; vel flore sub uno
Ceu gemina *Pæstani* rosæ per jugera regnant.
                                CLAUDIAN. De Nup. Hon. & Mar. 244.

(4) Ὅσα *Paestus* temeros πολισμα ἔλουσιν ως ἐνι ἀναγκαιον.
                                I. 251.

(5) Epit. Chron. Casinens. Muratori. Tom. II.

H   grant

grant of his Territories from the Pope (1). At his Invitation we find them failing from *Agropoli*, and landing at *Gaeta*. They did indeed help Docibilis to recover his Territories from Pandenulf, but at the Expence of a confiderable Part, which they appropriated to their own Ufe; fettling themfelves on the North fide of the *Gariglioni*, where they kept poffeffion above forty Years; till at length a Confederacy was formed against them by the Princes of *Italy*, by which, in the Year 915, they were entirely defeated, and by a general Carnage, almoft extirpated from the Country (2).

Those *Saracens*, who remained at *Agropoli*, hearing of thefe Misfortunes of their Countrymen, and dreading the fame Fate themfelves, determined to quit *Italy*; and after fecuring the moft valuable Effects they were able to carry with them, fet fire to the Town of *Paftum*, by which it was entirely deftroyed. From its ruins Robert Guiscard, in the eleventh Century, carried off fine marble Columns and other Materials to *Salernum*, which he made ufe of in the Church he was building and dedicating to *St. Matthew* (3); fo truly has Mr. Pope defcribed the Caufes of the Deftruction of thefe and other noble Monuments of Antiquity.

> *Some felt the filent Stroke of mould'ring Age,*
> *Some hoftile Fury, fome religious Rage;*
> *Barbarian Blindnefs, Chriftian Zeal confpire,*
> *And Papal Piety, and Gothic Fire.*
>
> Epiftle to Mr. Addison.

From that Time, till very lately, thefe Ruins have lain defolate and unnoticed (4); but thofe Travellers who have, within thefe few Years, ventured fo far out of the common Road of Travelling to fee them, all agree that their Curiofity has been amply rewarded. The Village, almoft deftitute of Inhabitants, that contains them, is now called *Piefti*, about fifty Miles South-Eaft of *Naples*, feven from the River *Selo* (5), and half a Mile from the Sea. It is fituated in a wide and pleafant Plain, that commands an extenfive View. The Country is diverfified into Vallies, Hills and Mountains, all which form the moft beautiful and inchanting Profpects.

---

(1) Leo Oft. L. V. C. 44, 44.

(2) Muratori. T. II. p. 466.

(3) Il Trat. di *Luania* D. Giuseppe Antonini. Napol. 1745.

(4) The firft public Notice of them was, probably, no longer ago than 1745, by the Baron D. G. Antonini; and by the ingenuous and learned Abbé Winkleman.

(5) This is the ancient *Silaris*, mentioned by Virgil, on account of the Goddefs, which then infefted it, and ftill continues to do fo.

Eft Lucos *Silari* circa, ilicibufque virentem
Plurimus Alburnum volitans, cui Nomen Afilo
Romanum eft: aeftron Graii vertêre vocantes,
Afper, acerba fonans; quo tota exterrita fylvâ

Diffugiunt armenta, furit mugitibus aether,
Concuffam, Sylvamque, & Sicci fluta Tanagri.
Virg. Georg. III. 146.

The purifying Qualities of its Waters were celebrated by Aristotle, Strabo, Silius Italicus, and Pliny, who fay, Similiar to *Anthius Silaris* alias Surmaven non vfquam modo innotefca, verum et fufta liquidefcunt; alias flabilos' pora clan injicit. Hift. Nat. II. 103. But Columella tells us, that when he examined this Property to the Inhabitants once it, they laughed at thofe Fables of Antiquity. Ruf. P. 1253. Though this faithful Geographer was upon the Spot, he feems to have minded his Bufinefs as a Geographer only; as it does not appear from any thing he has faid, that thefe magnificent Ruins made any Impreffion on him.

The Walls of it are still so entire, that they may be traced through the whole Extent, which is near three Miles; they are about twenty Feet high and eighteen thick, built with large Stones (1), which are nicely fitted, and laid one upon another, without Cement (2). Where the Openings now are, were probably the Gateways, which seem to have been four opposite to each other, one of which towards the South is still standing. A great Number of Towers, placed at no great Distance from one another, make Part of the Wall. Those nearest the Gates greatly exceed the others in Magnitude. They have Apertures, or small Openings only towards the City; the Structure of them seems not to be of equal Antiquity with the Walls. Within the Walls are to be seen the Remains of three large public Buildings, pretty entire, and others much less so, of an Amphitheatre and some Baths. The Remains of Buildings near the Sea, are the Ruins of the Port of *Pæstum*, being called to this Day *Il Porto*, The Port. They are now partly covered by the Sea. Without the Walls are the Remains of an Aqueduct, which brought Water to the City from the neighbouring Mountain; considerable Vestiges of this Aqueduct may be seen in the Road from *Capaccio Nuova* to *Trentenara*. This Aqueduct was necessary, as the little River which runs by the Walls of the Town has a brackish disagreeable Taste, and therefore called by the Inhabitants *Fiume Salso*. It continues, as in Strabo's Time, to stagnate in Marshes (3), by which the Air is rendered unwholesome; but was the Place to be again inhabited, these Marshes might be easily drained, and the Waters carried off to the Sea in their proper Channel; as, undoubtedly, must have been the Case, when the *Sybarites* were in Possession; of whose Taste, Wealth and Grandeur, the Monuments of Art, still remaining within the Walls of *PÆSTUM*, cannot fail of inspiring even at this Time of Day, very magnificent Ideas.

---

(1) This, and all the Stone in general, made use of about the City, particularly that of which the three Buildings are composed, has been dug out of the adjacent Mountains; it is of a rough porous Kind, and full of extraneous Bodies.

(2) Dr. Tancred Robinson, in a short Account of his Travels, published in the Philosophical Transactions, No. 349, says, " I observed in many of the Ruins about Rome and Naples, the great Stones, laid close and wedged very fast with little or no Cement."

(3) These are properly the Marshes mentioned by Plutarch in his Life of Crassus, which were in his Time filled, sometimes with fresh, and sometimes with salt Water.

Ἐχρῆτο μὲν οὖν ὁ Κράσσος, μὰ λᾶθαι τῆς ἐμᾶι τοι Συρζίονας τὴν ἱαι Περρον ὅλασινς. Διαἴδωι δὲ καλλον ἰφηνετζαι δια χρον γινομϊμη γλααινσαν, οὐ καλῆς ὠμοχρους καὶ κολῆς.

Itaque simul Cassius statim imperio Syriarum Romam ratores; verum confirmatus est, quod mihi ex disfortione descriviffent ab illo, et castra seorsum ad stagnum posuissent Limanam; quod certis temporibus variari ferunt, ac modo dulce, modo salsam nec potabile fieri.

PLUTARCH. in Crass.

I

A

D E S C R I P T I O N

OF THE

T E M P L E S.

M A N Y have thought that the *Greeks* borrowed their Rudiments of Art from the *Egyptians*, but we find they had very little Opportunity of learning the Principles of Architecture from them; for, before the Reign of King Psammeticus, the Entrance into *Egypt* was forbid to all Strangers. The Journey which the wife Men of *Greece* took into *Egypt*, then efteemed the Seat of Wifdom and the Sciences, was chiefly to learn from them, the Laws, Cuftoms and Government of that celebrated ancient Nation (1), the Arts having been cultivated, in *Greece*, long before that Period.

---

(1) Strabo, Lib. X. P. 482.

K

We

We find that these People set out upon the most simple Principles, whence it may be concluded, that they did not borrow their Ideas of Art from other Nations; but were themselves, as they assert, the original Inventors.

The *Greeks* having laid the Foundation of their Grandeur, what remained was, to complete the Superstructure with Stability and Magnificence. Their wise Men and Poets began the Work, and their Artists contributed, by their various Talents, to the Execution of this Design; they establishing an Eternity of Fame by their admirable Performances, that command universal Attention; and record to latest Posterity, their Dignity, their Opulence and Power.

The Graces took their Birth in *Greece*, and the Arts were carried to Perfection; when Reason, in conjunction with Liberty, enlightened and polished this charming Region. Its Constitution and Government were extremely favourable to Liberty, the great Nurse of Arts (1); which, joined to the happy Influence of the Climate, and the Esteem and Consideration in which Artists were then held, put the Powers of the Mind upon their utmost Stretch, and gave the highest Perfection to the Arts. The Use then made of Art was solely to great and noble Ends; it being applied chiefly to their Deities, and other sacred Purposes, and to whatever else was most useful and ornamental. The wealthy Citizens believed, that the best use they could make of their Riches, was to shew their Regard for the Arts, by encouraging and recompensing Artists; and those Citizens rendered themselves illustrious, by erecting public Edifices in a Taste equal to their Magnificence (2).

All Historians agree, that Architecture took its Rise in *Greece*; and that the Doric Order here described, on account of the shortness of its Columns, and the simplicity of the Entablature and Capital, comes the nearest to the Origin of Architecture: and what is here advanced appears the more probable, as these Columns have no Bases.

The Doric Order took its Rise from the simple Construction of the *Grecian* Huts, which were supported by the Trunks of Trees; in Imitation whereof, the first Idea of Columns was borrowed. These improving by Degrees, extended in Process of Time, over a great Part of the Universe; and gave rise to all the rest. This Order being the first and most ancient of all, and retaining more of the Structure of the primitive Huts than any other, it has also undergone the greatest Changes in its Proportions. We shall only consider it here in its first State, as being to our Purpose. The Columns were in general extremely short; they not having any fixed Rules to determine

---

(1) **Look upon** *Greece* under its Two States, and you would think its Inhabitants lived under different Climates, and under different Heavens, from those so praised; so opposite are the Geniuses which are formed under *Turkish* Slavery and *Grecian* Liberty.

ADDISON *Spect.* Vol. IV. No. 288.

(2) Histoire de l'Art chez les Anciens.

WINKLEMAN, Tom. I. P. 222, &c.

                                                    their

their Proportions. This appears from these Temples at *Pæstum*, which are not five Diameters in height.

These Ruins, though of the earliest *Grecian* Antiquity, are the most entire of any known; their Solidity having even refisted the destructive Power of Time. By the Taste and Proportion of these Buildings, and their Resemblance to those in Upper *Egypt* (1), it is evident that they are of the highest Antiquity.

The Silence of Historians, with regard to these Edifices, confirms us in the Opinion, how little we know concerning many Passages and Periods of an early or remote Date: But with respect to this Place, it is fully compensated by the Remains of the Temples; they themselves being Vouchers of their Antiquity. How far the Taste and Manner of the Architecture may throw a light upon the Age wherein they were built, is left to the Determination of the Reader.

The Gate towards the South, Letter D, in the general View, Plate I (2), is still fubfisting, and almost entire. On the Arch, upon the Key-stone facing the Country, there seems to have been a *Syren* or *Mermaid* in Basso-relievo. This probably alludes to the Reverence in which they were held by the *Posidonians*, as *Syrens* were said to inhabit all that Coast (3). This Opinion prevailing strongly at that Time, as we find by VIRGIL, OVID, and others (4), and *Posidonia* being a maritime Town, it is not unlikely its Inhabitants sacrificed to those supposed *Syrens*, in order to be preserved from Storms and Shipwrecks; but this is given as mere Conjecture. Upon the Key-stone, on the other Side of the Arch towards the City, there seems to have been a Figure; but it is so much defaced by Time, that there is no knowing, with any Certainty, what it was.

We are to observe, that in the View of the City, taken from under the Arch, Plate III. the Painter has ventured to make Breaks in the Wall, on the Right-hand Side, purposely to render the Prospect the more agreeable, and to shew the Hexastyle Peripteral Temple to greater Advantage. This is a Licence that is ever pardonable, when it makes no Difference in reality, as it throws the Objects into a more pleasing Form.

The chief Antiquities within the Walls of this City, are reduced to three superb Temples, and to the Remains of the Amphitheatre. These certainly were the Work of

---

(1) Pocock's Travels, Vol. I. P. 216.

(2) See Plate IV. and V.

(3) The Islands of the *Syrens* were near *Posidonia*.

(4) Jamque adeo scopulos *Sirenum* advecta subibat,
Difficiles quondam, multorumque offibus albos:
Tum rauca assiduo longe sale saxa sonabant.
Æn. Lib. 5. V. 864.
Cymothoe simul & *Triton* adnixus acuto

Detrudunt naves scopulo; levat ipse tridenti,
Et vastas aperit syrtes, & temperat æquor.
Ibid Lib. 1. V. 148.
Utque celer venias, virides *Nereïdas* oro.
OVID. Epist. V. 57.
Sirenum dedit una suum & memorabile nomen
Parthenope muris Acheloïs, æquore cujus
Regnare diu cantus, cum dulce per undas
Exitium miseris canerat non prosper a Nautis.
SIL. ITAL. L. 12.

the

the *Sybarites*, that rich, expensive, and voluptuous People; especially, if we conclude these Edifices to have been Temples, as the Abbé MAZOCHI (1), and the Marquis BERARDO GALIANI observe (2). It is well known that the *Greeks* were vastly magnificent and expensive in their Temples; but supposing these to have been only Porticos or Colonades, it is well known that the like Profusion was also bestowed upon them. They are now called, by the *Italians*, LI SEGGI DI PESTO.

As there are no Traces left whereby we may form a certain Judgment to what Deities these Temples were dedicated, for the sake of Distinction we shall therefore term them according to the Nature of their Construction; as for Example; the Temple, Letter A, in the general View, Plate I, we shall call the Hexastyle Ipetral Temple: the second, B, the Hexastyle Peripteral Temple: and the third, C, the Pseudodipteral Temple, or Basilica, it still remaining a Doubt to what Purpose this Building was applied.

THE three Temples are of the Doric Order, built of a hard coarse Stone, taken from the Quarries in the Mountain above *Cappacio Vechio* (3). Their Pillars are fluted, very shallow, to a sharp Edge, in the Manner described by VITRUVIUS, who says, that the *Greeks* adorned the Doric Column with a particular kind of shallow Flutings, whose Curvatures are described from the Center of a geometrical Square; no Interval or Fillet being left between them. The Number of Flutings to these Columns are twenty (4). Most of the ancient Columns were formed in this Manner, and were generally employed by the *Greeks*, in Works of the most remote Antiquity. The Columns diminish from the Foot of the Shaft, and this is esteemed the most natural and graceful (5). This Method was almost universally followed by the Ancients, in all the Orders (6). These Columns are without Bases, or any Plinth to raise them above the Ground; in Imitation of the Trees used in the first Buildings (7).

THEY

(1) In his Commentaries on the *Heraclean Tables*.

(2) In his Edition of VITRUVIUS, P. 103 and 113.

(3) Formerly this Mountain was called *Calumnum*, or *Calvetium*; and is distinguished for a memorable Battle, in the Year of *Rome* 676, where CRASSUS defeated the Army of SPARTACUS the Gladiator, near this Place.
CRASSUS fughterrant bello apud *Calumarum* educturus militem adversus CASTUM & CANIMECUM, duces *Gallorum*, XII cohortes cum C. PROMTINO, & cum Qy. MARCIO RUFFO legatis post montem circumissit, quæ, quum commisso jam prælio, a tergo clamore sublato, decurrissent, ita luderunt hostes, ut ubique fugam pro pugna capesserent.
FRONTINE Stratag. L. II. C. 4.

(4) Columnas (Doricas) autem striari XX striis oportet, quæ si planæ erunt, angulos habeant viginti designatos: sin autem excaventur, sic est forma facienda: ita uti quam magnum est Intervallum striæ, tam magnis striaturæ partibus latitudini quadratum, deformetur: in medio autem quadrato circini normam collocetur, & agatur linea rotundationis, quæ quadrationis angulos tangat, & quantum erit ea curvatura inter rotundationem & quadraturam,

deformationis, statuatur ad formam excaventur; ita Doricæ columnæ sui generis striaturæ habebit perfectionem.
Lib. IV. C. 3.
SCAMOZZI blames this Manner for its want of Stability; the projecting Angles between the Flutings being easily worn, and very subject to moulder.

(5) CHAMBERS's Civil Architecture, P. 17.

(6) The Columns of the *Pantheon*, those of the Temples of *Pola*, of *Jupiter Stator*, of *Antoninus* and *Faustina*, of *Concord*; of *Tivoli's* Arch, of *SEPTIMIUS's* Portico, of MARCELLUS's Theatre in *Rome*, all diminish in the same Manner.

(7) Ita unumquemque rei & Locorum, & Generis, & Ordinum proprium tueatur.——E quibus rebus, & a majoribusque fabri, in lapidea & marmoreis ædium facrarum ædificationibus artifices dispositiones eorum scalpturis sunt imitati, & eas inventiones persequendas putaverunt; ideo quod antiqui fabri quodam in loco ædificantes, cum ita ab interioribus parietibus ad extremas partes tigna prominentia habuissent collocata, intertignia fixerunt, supraque coronas & fastigia venustiore specie fabrilibus operibus ornaverunt.
VITRUV. Lib. IV. C. 2.
Many

THEY are of ſhorter Dimenſions than the cuſtomary Proportion generally aſſigned to that Order (1); this Diſproportion, (if we may be allowed the Expreſſion) is not very ſtriking at firſt ſight, from the uncommon Hugeneſs of their Bulk; the Characteriſtic of the male Appearance properly belonging to the Doric Order; this having a grave, robuſt and maſculine Aſpect, called by SCAMOZZI, *Herculean*; and as if intended originally to repreſent manly Strength and Beauty (2).

THE Duration indeed of theſe Buildings, for ſo many Ages, may be aſcribed, in ſome Meaſure, to the exceſſive Thickneſs of the Columns in Proportion to their Height, which muſt neceſſarily have added greatly to their Solidity. All of them are much in the ſame Taſte, there being ſcarce any Difference between them, except in the Pſeudodipteral Temple, in which there is a Foliage under the Ovolo.

The HEXASTYLE HYPÆTHRAL, *or* IPETRAL TEMPLE.

THE Hexaſtyle Ipetral Temple, in the general View, Plate I. Letter A. (3) is *Amphiproſtylos* (4), as VITRUVIUS calls it, Lib. III. C. 1. Amphiproſtyle, that is to ſay, two Proſpects, or equal Fronts, having ſix Columns in each Front, and fourteen on either Side, including thoſe of the Angles (5). The Intercolumniations here are eight Feet two Inches four Lines and a half. The Ancients were of opinion that a great Number of Columns round their Temples, ſeparated by ſmall Intercolumniations, contributed to the Grandeur and Solidity of their Edifices. Theſe Columns are ſix

---

Many are of opinion, that the Addition of a Baſe to the Doric Shaft, is an Innovation, contrary to the fixe Intention of the Ancients. Vitruvius likewiſe makes it without one; the Baſe, according to him, has been firſt employed in the Ionic.

The only Inſtance we have of this among the Ancients, is in the firſt Order of the *Coliſeum* at *Rome*, built by VESPASIAN.

Monſ. de CHAMBRAY obſerves, that the Cuſtom of employing a Baſe, in the Doric Order, in oppoſition to all ancient Authorities, hath from a ſtrong and unaccountable Idea of Beauty, prevailed; but which, when examined, will appear falſe and extravagant.

The Remarks made by Monſ. LE CLERC, on the above Monſ. de CHAMBRAY, where he ſpeaks of the Doric Columns having no Baſe, are very judicious. Perſons of ſiſte (?)ſigh this Author will grant, that a Baſe not only gives a Grace to the Column, but is of real Uſe, by ſerving to keep it firm on its Plan; and that if Columns, without Baſes, are now the mode, it is a Mark of the Wiſdom of the Architect, rather than an Indication of his being governed by Prejudice.

CHAMBRAY's Civil Architecture, P. 20.

(1) PLATE five, L. VI. C. 23. that the Doric Order had, in Height, ſix Diameters of its lower Thickneſs.

Theſe ſtill remain at *Grecce* the Ruins of Doric Temples, whoſe Proportions are ſo ſhort, that they have not ſix Diameters in Height. One at *Thericus*, ten Leagues from *Athens*, and another at *Corinth*, which is certainly the moſt ſingular, thoſe Columns being the fourth of any now known; they not having four Diameters in Height; their Thickneſs being about ſix Feet four Inches, and their Height about twenty-three Feet

eleven Inches. The firſt of theſe Temples has the Columns ſmooth, the other fluted.

Mémoire. de la Grece, LE ROY, P. 1 and 5, Second Part.

(2) Dorica columna virilis corporis proportionem, & firmitatem, & venuſtatem in ædificiis præſtare cœpit.

VITRUV. L. IV. C. 1.

This Order was generally employed in Temples dedicated to MINERVA, MARS, and HERCULES.

(3) See Plates VI. VII. VIII. and IX.

(4) Amphiproſtylos omnia habet ea, quæ Proſtylos; præterеaque habet in poſtico æd numerum modum columnas, & faſtigium.

(5) In eadem ride duplex longitudo operis ad latitudinem. Namque quæ columnarum duplicationem fecerunt, ceraſtſ? videntur, quod unam ſuperdimenſion in longitudine pluſquam oportet procurrere videntur.

Lib. III. C. 3.

As this Temple has only ſix Columns in Front, and fourteen on the Sides, its Length is more than twice its Breadth. The uſual Plan of the *Grecian* Temples was a rectangular Parallelogram; and their lateral Walls were continued without Interruption, from the Antæ of the Portico, to the Poſticus or back Front. This Proportion ſeems to have been generally followed by the Ancients; which is confirmed by the Dimenſions of the Temple of *Minerva* at *Athens*, it having eight Columns in Front, and ſeventeen on the Sides. Alſo by that of *Theſeus*, in the ſame Place, which has ſix Columns in Front, and thirteen on the Sides. Likewiſe by the famous Temple of *Jupiter Olympius*, which PAUSANIAS ſays, had ninety-five Feet in Front, and two hundred and thirty Feet in Length. Theſe Temples greatly exceed thoſe that were afterwards built by the *Romans*, as VITRUVIUS obſerves.

M   Feet

Feet eight Inches and two Lines in Diameter, refting on a Platform or Bafement raifed above the Ground, to which we afcend by three Steps (1), that go round the Temple, in like Manner. They are four Feet nine Inches in Height; whence it may be concluded, that the *Greeks* attended more to proportion the Steps which went round their Temples to the Dimenfions of the Architecture, than to the Eafinefs of the Afcent: and this Meafure agrees nearly with the Proportion mentioned by VITRUVIUS.

THE Capitals confift of a plain Abbacus, and an Ovolo under it, with three Annulets (2). The Echinus of the Capital is rounded a little, but greatly refembles that of the Temple of *Corinth* (3). Inftead of Aftragals they have three Cavets, or Hollows, feparate from each other, and the Flutings are continued through them to the lower Annulet. Monf. LE ROY fays, " It appears, from all the Doric Columns which " are found in *Greece*, without Aftragals, that this Ornament took its Rife from the " Ionic, to which it was applied by the *Greeks*; and, I apprehend, the *Romans* were " the firft who introduced it in the Doric Order (4)."

THE Entablature is maffy and high, becaufe thefe Columns are much ftronger and larger in Proportion, than thofe of all the other Orders, and the Simplicity and Strength of the Architrave gives it a fuperiour Degree of Solidity: It confifts of only one Fafcia, with the Tænia Fillet, and fix Drops, which are conical, and not piramidal. All the Architraves are now fubfifting, and of a Size correfpondent to the Diminution of the Columns, which is very confiderable towards the Top. The Architrave and Frize project a little beyond the upper Part of the Column, contrary to the eftablifhed Rule of VITRUVIUS (5). This was the conftant Practice in the Conftruction of the *Grecian* Temples, and continued till the Time of AUGUSTUS.

THE Diftribution of the Doric Frize, obliged the *Greeks* to make the Intercolumniations of the Angles a little fmaller than the others; they chufing that the Frize fhould finifh the Angles by Triglyphs, and not by a Demy Metope (6), as was afterwards the Practice of the *Romans*.

---

(1) Sigraque rerum prolixe extruuntur fub columnis dimidio evalleretur, quam columnæ funt futuræ, uti firmiora fint inferiora fuperioribus, quæ flexibata appellantur, non emittunt onera: fpirarumque projectura non immittunt extra fulfum. Namque cum ab octo pede priores gradus afcendatur, item in fummo templo quiuua erit ponenda.

Lib. III. C. 3.

(2) Craffitudo capituli dividatur in partes tres, e quibus una plinthus cum cymatio fiat — Altera echinus, tertia cum annulis.

Lib. IV. C. 3.

(3) *Monum. de la Grec*, LE ROY, P. 42.

(4) Il paroît même par tout les Ordres Doriques, que l' on trouve en Grec, qui font privés d' aftragales, que cet ornement a pris naiffance avec l' Ordre Ionique, auquel, comme je le fais voir, les Grec l'avoient un aftragale, & je fuppofe que ce fut les Remains font les premiers qui l'ayent appliqué à l' Ordre Dorique.
Monum. de la Grec, P. 2. Partie Seconde.

(5) Item epiftylii latitudo ima refpondeat hypotrachelio fummæ columnæ.

Lib. IV. C. 3.

(6) La diftribution de la frize Dorique, força les Grec de faire les entre-colonnes des angles des leurs Temples Doriques, un peu plus petits que les autres, parce qu' ils vouloient que les frifes Doriques fuffent terminées à leurs angles par des triglyphes, & non par par des demi-métopes.
Monum. de la Grec, LE ROY, P. 7. Partie Seconde.
Tum projecturæ tignorum, quantum eminebant, ad lineam et perpendiculum parietum perfecuerunt. quæ fpatia cum cavernula ita effet, tabellas ita formatas, uti nunc fiunt triglyphi, contra tignorum præcifiones in fronte fixerunt. fe ora cæra cærulea deplanxerunt, ut præcifionis tignorum occultam non offenderent vifum. Ita divifiones tignorum occultæ triglyphorum difpofitione, intertignium & opam habere in Doricis operibus cœperunt.

VITRUV. Lib. IV. C. 2.

SOME

Some of the Triglyphs, and the Metopes (1), are still distinguished in the Frize.
The Angles are terminated by a Triglyph (2), (as are all the Doric Temples in *Greece*)
the Face of which is even with the Architrave.

THERE are no Mutules in the Pediment under the Corona; and VITRUVIUS obferves,
that the *Greeks* never employed either Modillions or Dentils in the horizontal Cornices of
their Pediments; both of them reprefenting Parts in the Conftruction of a Roof, which
cannot poffibly appear in that View (3). This and the Peripteral Temple have the
common Doric Cornice.

THE Afcent to the Pronaos is by three Steps; and farther within appear the Traces
of the Wall which enclofed the Cella, or Body of the Temple. But there now remain
only the infulated Antæ (4), or Pilafters of the Angles, which divided the Inner, from
the Pronaos or Anti Temple. Thefe, together with two Columns in a Line with the
Pilafters, and fronting the two middle Columns of the Portico, ferved, (as we may fay)
to inclofe the former. In the interior Part of the Temple, from two Rows of feven
Columns, now ftanding, of the fame Order, it is evident that there muft have been
another Portico within. Thefe Columns are four Feet feven Inches two Lines and a half
in Diameter. They have Architraves, whereon are placed a fecond Order of fmaller
Columns, that have only fourteen Flutings (5), likewife Doric, and which fupport
their proper Architraves (6). With regard to this Edifice, we may fafely venture to call
it an *Ipetral Temple*, when compared with that defcribed by VITRUVIUS in the firft
Chapter of his third Book, and called by him *Hypæthros* (7).

THIS Temple, in its exterior Form, greatly refembles that of THESEUS at *Athens* (8);
but bears the evident Marks of much more remote Antiquity, from the Nature of its

Conftruction.

Conftruction. The Columns are confiderably fhorter, and the Entablature much larger. Thofe of the Temple of Thefeus have fix Diameters in Height; as have all the Edifices erected at *Athens*, at the Time when the Arts flourifhed in that City.

The HEXASTYLE PERIPTERAL TEMPLE.

THE fecond Temple to be defcribed, is the Hexaftyle Peripteral, in the general View, Plate I. Letter B (1). This is alfo Amphiproftyle, but confiderably fmaller than the other, and ftands at fome Diftance from it. This has likewife fix Columns in each Front, and thirteen on either Side (2), including the angular Columns. They are four Feet one Inch and two Lines in Diameter, raifed on a Bafement of three Steps, like the former. The Intercolumniation, of thofe in the Fronts, is four Feet fix Inches three Lines and three Quarters, but thofe on the Sides are fmaller. In the Frize, fome of the Cavities are plainly diftinguifhed, wherein the Triglyphs muft have been placed; but which, either from the natural Decay of the Cement wherein they were laid, or from their having been of Marble or of Bronze, were forced out by Violence, and carried away for the Sake of the Materials. This probably was the Cafe here, as many of the ancient Temples had Triglyphs of Bronze.

FARTHER in, appear the Remains of five broken Columns, being Part of thofe belonging to the Pronaos; to which we afcend by three Steps, in the fame Manner as in the former Temple. The Ruins of the Walls, which enclofed the Cella or Middle of the Temple, are feen in many Places; which, with the outer Portico, and the remaining Parts of the Columns of the Pronaos or Porch, may altogether induce us to believe, that this Edifice muft have been a Temple of that Sort which is defcribed and called by VITRUVIUS, *Peripteros*, Lib. III. C. 1. (3).

The PSEUDODIPTERAL TEMPLE, or BASILICA.

THE laft Edifice to be defcribed is the Pfeudodipteral Temple or Bafilica, in the general View, Plate I. Letter C (4), which is alfo Amphiproftyle, and at a fmall Diftance from the firft. In this Building there are nine Columns in each Front, and eighteen on the Flanks, including the angular Columns of both Fronts (5), placed on a Bafement, to which we afcend by three Steps, like the others. The Intercolumniations here are four Feet ten Inches eight Lines and a Quarter. Near the outer Colonade, going further

---

(1) See Plates XIII. XIV. XV. XVI.

(2) Pteromatos enim ratio, & columnarum elarum ædem difpofitio ideo eft inventa, ut afpectus propter afperitatem intercolumniorum haberet auctoritatem. Præterea fi & imbrium aquam vis occupaverit, & inaerfuerit horfaum multitudinem, ut habeat in æde circaque cellam cum lacunario liberam morem.

VITRUV. Lib. III. C. 2.

(3) Peripteros autem erit, quæ habebit in fronte, & poftico fenas columnas, in lateribus cum angularibus undenas: ita ut fint

lae columnae collocatae, ut intercolumnii latitudinis intervallum fit a parietibus circum ad extremos ordines columnarum, habeatque ambulationem circa cellam ædis.

(4) See Plates XVIII. XIX. XX. XXI.

(5) This Temple, though it has no more than twice the Number of Columns in Length, than in the Fronts, has yet more than twice its Breadth; becaufe the Intercolumniations, on the Sides, are larger than thofe in the Front.

in, we find the Remains of a Wall, which, with the infulated Pilafters and Columns,
form an Enclofure as in the firft Temple, except only, that here there are three Columns
now exifting, which range in a Line with the Pilafters that fupport an Architrave, and
front the middle Columns of the Portico. But what is moft extraordinary, is, a Range
of Columns which divide the Cella, and runs from End to End, through the Middle;
as is feen by three of them now ftanding with their Architrave.

This Edifice may be faid to exhibit the direct Figure of a Temple, in all its
Parts; and efpecially of the Sort defcribed by Vitruvius, and by him called *Pfeudodipteros*,
in the firft Chapter of his third Book (1).

It is very furprizing, and muft neceffarily employ the Attention of thofe much
converfant in Arts, to find an odd Number of Columns in the Fronts, which confift
(as was obferved) of nine in each; and ftill more fo, at feeing the Range placed in
the Middle of the Edifice, which could not but obftruct the Sight, both from the
Door, and from the internal Part of the Building. Monf. Le Roy, in his Difcourfe
on the *Hiftory of Civil Architecture*, feems very judiciously to account for this Range
of Columns in the Middle. He fays, " The firft Temples which the *Grecians* built,
" becoming too fmall, occafioned by the Encreafe of the People who facrificed, the
" Architects erected larger; when perceiving that the Beams which compofed the Cieling,
" bent and over-ftrained their new Buildings; and, perhaps, not finding the Defect,
" till after the Edifices were finifhed: To remedy this they cut Trunks of Trees, when
" placing them perpendicular at equal Diftances under the Beam, which extended the
" whole Length of the Temple, and fupported all the Crofs-Beams in the Middle; this
" muft have eafed the Edifice." Hence, probably, arofe the Idea of building a Temple
with an odd Number of Columns in the Fronts, and a Range running through the
Middle; and in a Note upon the above, He fays, " This Conjecture is founded on the
" Manner in which the Columns were at firft placed in the *Greek* Temples, from the
" Conftruction of two which are of the moft remote Antiquity, one of which is feen
" at *Pæftum* in *Italy*, an ancient City of *Magna Græcia*. This has a Range of Columns,
" in the infide, exactly in the Middle, in the Manner that we may fuppofe Columns
" were at firft placed in their Buildings. The other is at *Egina* (2), which has five
" Columns at the fecond Portico of both its Fronts, and confequently a Column in the

---

(1) Pfeudodipteros autem fic collocatur, ut in fronte, & poftico
fint columnæ octonæ, in lateribus cum angularibus quindenæ.
Sunt autem pariotes cellæ contra quaternas columnas medianas in
fronte, & poftico: ita duorum intercolumniorum, & imæ craffitudinis
columnæ fpatium erit a parietibus circa ad extremos ordines
columnarum.

—— Hermogenes, qui etiam primus octaftylum, pfeudodipterive
rationem invenit: ex dipteri enim ædis fymmetria fuftulit
interiores ordines columnarum XXXVIII: eaque ratione fumptus
operifque compendia fecit; is in medio ambulationi laxamentum
egregie circa cellam fecit, de afpectuque nihil imminuit, fed

fine defiderio fupervacuorum conftructi auctoritatem totius operis
diftributione.

VITRUV. Lib. III. C. 2.

(2) An ifland inhabited by the *Dorians*, where the Artifts
feem to have longer preferved the ancient Manner of Building,
than others.

HERODOT. Lib. VIII. P. 43.

There are two Temples of this Kind, of a moft ancient Date;
the one at *Kemombu*, in *Upper Egypt*, defcribed by NORDEN,
(*Voyage d'Egypte & de Nubie*) P. 187. Pl. CXXVII. where is a
Range of Columns through the Middle; and another called the
Temple of the Serpent KNUPHIS, P. 195, Pl. CXXXII.

O

" Middle.

" Middle.   A Circumstance that seems to authorise my Opinion, is, the Origin of the
" Word *Columen*, that signifies Column, which, according to VITRUVIUS (1), took its Name
" from a Piece of Wood called *Culmen*, placed under, and supporting the Ridge of the
" Roof. (2).". It does not seem to exhibit the Form of a Basilica, because its Portico
is on the outside; whereas those described by VITRUVIUS were in the inside.   Nor can
we suppose it to have been simply a Portico, as the Ruins of the Walls of the Cella
are still visible.   All its other Parts, (the odd Number of Pillars in the Fronts excepted,
and the abovementioned Range of Columns, in the Middle) seem Characteristics of a
Temple only (3); unless we may conjecture, that as *Pæstum* was a maritime City,
the Edifice in question served, not only as a Basilica for the Administration of publick
Justice,   but at the same Time, a Place for transacting the Affairs of Commerce.
However, it is not improbable that this Edifice (which seems the most ancient of
the three) was a Temple dedicated to NEPTUNE; a Deity, whom we may imagine, the
Posidonians had in the highest Veneration, as is evident, from the frequent Repetition of
his Figure on so many of their Coins.   But in this Uncertainty, and till farther
Discoveries shall have been made with Regard to this Edifice, we must leave the whole
to the Determination of the judicious Reader.

ALMOST in the Center of the City stand the Ruins of the Amphitheatre, in
the general View, Plate I. Letter F; one hundred and seventy five Feet long, and
one hundred and twenty Feet wide.   All the Caves are still subsisting, and over them
are seen the Remains of ten Rows of Seats.   In one of the Extremities is an impending
Arch, which appears to have been one, (of the many) that inclosed the whole Circuit,
and supported the second Flight of Steps.

BETWEEN the Amphitheatre and the Ipetral Temple, are the Ruins of another
large Building.   This is entirely level with the Ground, except the Remains of a few
broken Columns still standing, which make it impossible for us to form any certain
Conjecture what Sort of Edifice this might have been; though it probably was a Theatre,
as these Ruins occupy a large Space of Ground.

OF the various other Antiquities less worthy of Note, we shall not give any Account,
as our Intentions were to confine ourselves solely to the Description of the Temples.
Were proper Researches made, and Persons employed to dig about the Amphitheatre,
and near the great Temple, there is no Doubt but that they would be richly
compensated for their Trouble and Expence; and some Inscriptions discovered, which
might enable the Publick to form a decisive Judgment on these Edifices, whose very
Names, at present, Time hath totally buried in Oblivion.

---

(1) Columen in summo fastigio culminis, unde et columnæ
dicuntur.
              VITRUV. L. IV. C. 2.

(2) *Adunan. de la Grec, Discout for l'Histoire de l'Architecture
Civile.* Page 10.
(3) Il Trutt. di *Lucanio*, D. G. ANTONINI.

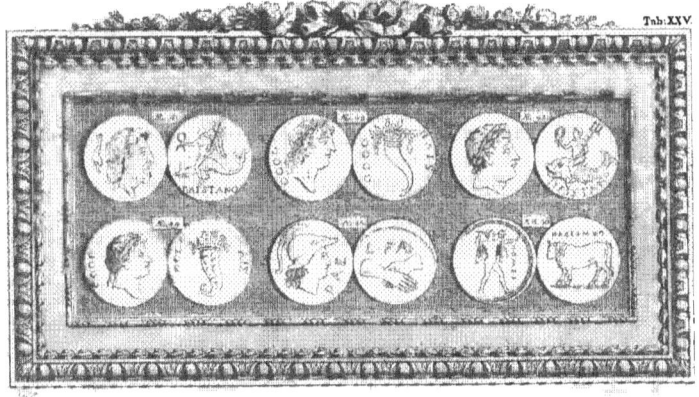

A

DISSERTATION

ON THE

COINS and MEDALS

OF

POSIDONIA, or PÆSTUM.

HE *Grecian* and *Afiatic* Cities made Ufe of Money long before the Time of ALEXANDER (1). It is uncertain whether this Prince ord.red that all the current Coin in his Empire fhould bear his Name, but we know that his Succeffors, and alfo the *Romans* afterwards, directed that the Coins of fome Cities fhould only have the Name of the Prince who governed them put

---

(1) We are beholden to the ingenious and learned Abbé | in the *Mem. de l'Acad. des Infcrip.* Tom. XXIV, & XXVI.
BARTHELEMY for a great Part of the following curious Remarks, |

thereon;

thereon; this was difpenfed with us to other Cities; and they fometimes agreed that the Names of the City and Prince fhould be joined together on the fame Coin.

THE Medals ftruck by thefe Cities furnifh us with many ufeful Lights in Geography, and help to explain the Cuftoms and Religion of the Country where they were coined, the Nature of its Government, and the various Changes it underwent. But as thefe Medals have feldom any Dates, and one hardly finds on them any of thofe great Events recorded in Hiftory, one can reap but little Advantage from them, if fome Method is not found out to afcertain the Time when they were ftruck.

WE have been long accuftomed to the Diftinction eftablifhed between Coins and Medals, fo that when we look upon ancient Medals, we are apt to confider them as Records of the Glory of the Perfons whofe Names they bear; or, as Monuments confecrated to their Memories: And this Prejudice, if it be one, feems to be favoured by the equivocal Terms ufed by fome Antiquaries. But we muft remember, that what we now call Medals, were, with the Ancients, fimply Money; excepting fome of the Imperial Medals, and even thofe are rather doubtful: The *Greeks*, and efpecially thofe prior to the *Roman* Empire, did not ftrike their Coin with an Intention of tranfmitting to Pofterity the Actions of Heroes, the good Deeds of Princes, or the Magnificence of Cities; for the Emblems they were furnifhed with, were taken from the Statues and Symbols of the Gods whom they adored, the Production of the Climates in which they lived, the Cuftoms and Traditions of each Country, with other Singularities peculiar to the Situation of thofe Places. Hence the Moneyers were fupplyed with Types, which they often repeated, and at length they became common to many Princes and various Towns. Some Medals of MITHRIDATES, King of *Pontus*, ftruck at *Amafus*, reprefent a *Pegafus*, the Device which that City often ufed upon its Money. An Eagle difplayed is feen on almoft all the Coins of the Kings of *Egypt*; thofe of ALEXANDER *the Great* have not any particular Reference to the remarkable Tranfactions of his Life. If upon his Coins, or thofe of other Princes, a Victory be fometimes reprefented, or triumphal Cars, thefe Devices are not explained by any Infcriptions; and there is Reafon to believe, that they were copied from other Monuments; at leaft, were not particularly intended to commemorate thofe Actions to which at firft View they feem to refer.

THE firft Money in ufe was probably only rough Pieces of Metal of irregular Shapes, without Device or Infcription, to which a Value was given in proportion to the Weight. In procefs of Time there was a Neceffity of impreffing Money with fome Mark, as well to diftinguifh it from Counterfeits, as to afcertain its Weight. The Motives that brought on this Alteration, induce us to believe that when an Impreffion was firft put on Coin, it was only a fingle Device, and that but on one Side; for we generally find on the Reverfe of thefe Coins a Hollow, which for the moft Part is not deeper than half a Line, either in the Middle or on the Sides: this was occafioned by the Face of the Block, or Matrice, on which they were ftruck, having fome little

Projections,

Projections, which served to keep the Metal steady and in its Place, while it received a second Blow, this Operation being then performed by the repeated Strokes of a Hammer.

If in the flourishing State of *Greece*, the Ancients had the Idea that Money was only designed to facilitate Commerce, what must we think of the Ages still further back, when they used only a single Impreffion on their Coin? The Authors of this Cuftom were lefs attentive to their own Glory than to the public Utility, and therefore chofe the fimpleft Methods of obtaining this End. They had very good Reafons for impreffing a Mark upon their Money, but none for putting one on both Sides; it was fufficient to have the Seal of Authority on one, to anfwer the intended Purpofe: and as in the Infancy of Printing they ufed only one Side of the Leaf, we may alfo conclude, that in the Beginning of Coinage, they only made Ufe of a fingle Device, or Impreffion, on one Side. This Confequence, fo fimple and natural, is confirmed by a Sort of Medals to which few Antiquaries have fufficiently attended; one Side of which is concave and the other in relief. If thefe Kind of Impreffions, fingular in Appearance, happened only on one or two Medals, we might feek no further for an Explanation than that of its being merely a Caprice, or Accident, of the Coiner; but we fee on many Medals of the earlieft Date, the evident Marks of the Cavities on one Side.

The firft Effays in Arts and Sciences have ever been crude, fimple and unpolifhed: The Knowledge of them muft be progreffive, and their Arrival at Perfection by very flow Degrees. This Art daily improving, the Artifts ornamented the hollow Parts of the lower Die, and at length, engraved thereon fometimes a Head, or repeated the fame Figure. See Plate XXIV. No. 1, 2, and 35. At other Times they put different Symbols, and this was the Origin of double Impreffions on Medals.

There are Medals of *Metapontum*, executed in the fame Manner, having on one Side the Head of a Bull, and on the other an Ear of Corn; on thofe of *Crotona* fometimes an Eagle is difplayed, and on the Reverfe a Tripod; this laft Device is found on fome Medals of this City, concave on one Side, and the fame Device, but not reverfed, in relief, on the other; from whence it follows, that thefe Medals were ftruck by two different Dies, one of which was hollow, and the other in relief. This Practice feems to have been the Confequence of the old concave Manner; for when the *Greeks* adopted the Ufe of double Impreffions on their Money, in the chief Cities of *Magna Græcia*, they did not entirely give up the Ufe of ftriking them with two Dies, one of which was in relief, and the other concave: inftead of the lower Die, as at firft made hollow, with fmall Projections in fome Part to keep the Metal fteady in ftriking, they engraved the Device in relief, which appears concave on the Medals. Poffibly they might have a particular Reafon for this, as the ufing of lefs Metal, a fmaller Quantity fufficing on this Occafion, than for thofe which were impreffed in relief on both Sides. Thefe Kind of Medals, for the moft Part, are extremely thin, which feems to confirm

Q   this

this Opinion.   They were chiefly ſtruck about four hundred Years before the Birth
of Chriſt.

THERE are alſo other Medals that have one Side hollow, which are found on the
moſt ancient of *Magna Græcia*.   Theſe have two Impreſſions, one convex and the other
concave.   They have ſome reſemblance to thoſe Medals which the Antiquaries call
Incuſers; they are not only found in the Series of the conſulary and imperial Medals,
but alſo among thoſe of the Kings and *Grecian* Cities.   See Plate XXIX, No. 49,
which is one of this Sort ſtruck at *Sybaris*.   However, they muſt not be confounded
together, as theſe laſt owe entirely to Chance, the Singularity that diſtinguiſhes them
from the others.   The Coiner forgetting to take out the Medal which had been ſtruck
between the two Dies, and putting in another Piece of Metal over that, it was preſſed
between the preceding Medal and the upper Die, by which it received the Impreſſion
of the ſame Device on one Side hollow, and the other in relief.

IT is certain that the Ancients were Strangers to the Uſe of the Fly-Preſs, as
appears by the Inſpection of their Coin, the Sides of which are always uneven, a Defect
proceeding from their Manner of Working, and ſtriking them with a Hammer, which
ſtretched out the Metal into irregular Shapes, paying no Regard to the Rim or Edge
of the Coin, but only to the Work that was upon it.   However imperfect this Method
might be, it was conſtantly practiſed in the *Grecian* Cities, as we may conclude
from a Number of *Greek* braſs Coins, ſtruck after the Time of ALEXANDER (1).

THE *Greeks* carried the Art of Engraving Medals to a high Degree of Perfection, becauſe
the Arts on which it depended were arrived at their Summit, and it was natural for
the Art of Engraving to advance with the Sciences of Painting and Sculpture.   The
Grecian Painters and Sculptors, who ſaw Beauty in its utmoſt Splendour and Delicacy,
when they had produced the moſt exquiſite Pieces in their different Branches, theſe the
Engravers had the Advantage of having before their Eyes, and, no Doubt, endeavoured
to imitate in the beſt Manner they could.   We do not find that the Ancients ever
diſtinguiſhed the Medal Engravers in the ſame Manner in which they honoured thoſe
Artiſts that tranſmitted their Fame to Poſterity.   Hiſtory, that gives us the Names of
many Painters, Sculptors, Architects, and alſo Engravers in precious Stones, has never
celebrated any Medal Engraver, unleſs it may be ſaid that theſe two laſt Profeſſions
were not formerly diſtinguiſhed from each other, and that the ſame Artiſts wrought
alternately in both.

---

(1) In *Italy*, ſo late as the Time of Pope CLEMENT VII,
Medals were ſtruck with a Hammer, and alſo by the Fly-Preſs.
BENVENTO CELLINI aſſures that he made uſe of both Methods
alternately. Notwithſtanding the laſt is much more exact and
certain, it was a long Time before the old Method was entirely
laid aſide.
The firſt Money in *England* ſtruck by the Fly-Preſs, was in
the Reign of Queen ELIZABETH, about the Year 1561;

but was diſcontinued till the Time of OLIVER CROMWEL,
1650. This Method was ſoon laid aſide, but afterwards was
revived by Monſ. BLONDEAU and the Monoyers in the Mint,
upon the Pattern Pieces of Coin engraved by the incomparable
SIMONS, though it was not eſtabliſhed by Authority till the
Reign of CHARLES the Second, 1663.

View of the Silver Coinage of *England*, SNELLING.

Tab XXIX

D E S C R I P T I O N

O F   T H E

C O I N S   and   M E D A L S (1).

HESE may be ranged under three Claſſes; firſt, thoſe of the moſt ancient Date, when the City was called *P O S I D O N I A*; ſecondly, thoſe inſcribed ΠΑΙΣΤ, after it was conquered by the *Lucanians*; thirdly, thoſe with a *Latin* Inſcription, after it came under the Power of the *Romans*.

IN the firſt Claſs, thoſe numbered 1, 2 and 35 are, undoubtedly, the moſt ancient, and remarkable as well for their being hollow on one Side, as for the Inſcription going from right to left, and for the ſingular Form of ſome of the Letters. The firſt is of Silver, in the Collection of the Duke of *Noia*, and is ſo like that, No. 35, of the

---

(1) The Medals being engraved as they came to Hand, is the Reaſon they could not be placed upon the Plates in their proper Order.

ſame

fame Metal in the imperial Cabinet at *Vienna*, that one would have fufpected the
Miftake of the firft Engraver had made the Difference, if the Editors had not expreffly
told us, that the Letters on one Side did not exactly anfwer to thofe on the other (1).
On this Medal we find NEPTUNE ftanding in the Act of darting his Trident; he is
almoft naked, except a fmall Drapery crofs his Shoulders.

WHEN afterwards it was found convenient to have a different Device for each Side
of the Medal, we find a Bull made ufe of for this Purpofe. The Connection between
NEPTUNE and this Animal is celebrated in moft of the old Writers; in HESIOD he is
called Ταυρος Ενναγγαις, and HESYCHIUS fays, Ταυρος, Ταυρεος, Ο Ποσειδων. The Reafon
generally affigned is, becaufe the Waves of the Sea roar like a Bull (2), but we will
try whether we cannot give a better Account of this Animal's appearing on one Side
of the old *Pofidonian* Medals, and alfo explain the Attitude in which NEPTUNE is
reprefented on the other.

THE *Græcian* Mythologifts (3) tell us, that NEPTUNE and MINERVA contending for
the Honour of the Naming and Patronage of *Attica*, *Jupiter* determined that it fhould
be given to that Deity who produced what, in the Judgment of twelve other Deities,
fhould be reckoned of moft Benefit to Mankind. That NEPTUNE ftriking the Earth
with his Trident, out of the Opening iffued a Horfe (4), whilft MINERVA caufed an
Olive Tree to fpring forth, to which the Prize was allotted.

IT is not eafy to feparate Truth from Falfehood in thefe Legends: That Difputes
fhould arife about the Honour of giving Name to a new planted Colony is not
improbable nor unufual; and we find PAUSANIAS, and other Writers, alluding to the
Conteft on this Occafion between the two Deities. As NEPTUNE, therefore, failed in
giving his Name to *Attica*, why may we not fuppofe, that he contented himfelf with
doing this to a City within the *Ifthmus*? Such a one we find there was, called
originally *P O S I D O N I A*, and afterwards *T R O E Z E*; from whence we have
already ftarted a Conjecture (5), that the firft *Greek* Settlers at *Pofidonia* may have been
derived. M. PELLERIN (6) has given us a Medal of *Trœze* with the head of NEPTUNE on
one Side, and a Trident on the Reverse, very like to that of *Pæftum*, engraved No. 47,
and if the more ancient Coins of *Trœze* could be recovered, we might poffibly find
them refembling the early ones of *Pofidonia*, with the Figure of NEPTUNE infculped
upon them in the Act of darting his Trident at the Earth.

PLUTARCH informs us, that THESEUS, who fignalized himfelf fo much in the civilizing
of *Athens*, and regulating its Government, among other Arts, for thefe Purpofes, introduced

---

(1) Eft numifma aureorum perpetuatum atque ubii pars averfa
.eft figura eadem concava eft fixere non refpondere emulno,
Numifmata Clariff. Cæfaris Vindobonenfis, Fol. 1764, P. 34.

(2) Δια τυ τον κυραλον εχει οι Ταυροι γας μυκωντας.
                              J. TZETZES *in Scholii*.

(3) APOLLODORUS, HYGINUS.

(4) Others fay a Lake.

(5) P. 9, Note 5.

(6) Recueil des Medailles de Peuples & de Villes. T. I, P. 132.

the stamping of Money, on which a Bull was insculped, for which PLUTARCH assigns various Reasons, leaving the Reader to take his Choice (1); JULIUS POLLUX also mentions this as the Device on the old *Athenian* Money, and uses a remarkable Expression for the Manner in which it was stamped, corresponding with that of PLUTARCH's, and both representing the Bull as insculped, or as we may more properly express it, embossed upon the Coin (2).

Now THESEUS, as we have already mentioned (3), was born at *Trœze*, and therefore we may suppose, that the useful Art, which he invented, of ascertaining the Value of Money, would not be long a Stranger to his native City; and that this Art, together with others, would be introduced into *Magna Grœcia*, by that joint Colony of *Acheans* and *Trœzenians*, who first founded *Sybaris* (4). Accordingly, the Device that appears on the few Medals of *Sybaris* yet discovered, is a Bull, and this embossed, or hollow on one Side, in the Manner described by PLUTARCH and POLLUX. The *Posidonians* derived from these, stamped their Money in the same Manner, first with the Image of their Patron Deity, and afterwards they added the Bull.

THE high Antiquity we have ascribed to these curious Medals, is further confirmed by the singular shape of some of the Letters, and the inscription going from right to left. The Shapes of the , the and the come much nearer the old *Phœnician* or *Samaritan* Characters (5), than those at present known or described, as CADMUS's Alphabet (6). And as this Alphabet was adopted from the East, so it should seem from these Medals, was the Manner of writing it from right to left. But a few ancient Inscriptions, yet remaining on Marbles, give us Reason to think, that this Method was never implicitly followed by the *Greeks*, but that they steered a Kind of a middle Course, by alternately ranging the Lines from right to left and left to right, in the same Manner as Oxen plough; thence called *Boustrophedon*. Whence also, possibly the Phrase *Exarare literas*, and the Word *Versus*. For, though it does not appear that the *Latins* ever adopted

(1) Ζωιλο ὃ ὁ Νηχηκος, BOTN ΣΤΚΑΓΑΡΛΣ, ὁ δη τος Μαγαδωπω ʼδωρις, ἐ διὰ τὰς ἄλλας χρὰσας, ὁ διὰ τησαριας της Βοαδος απομιασω.

Περεϰθι etiam numismatum, Bovem Insculptum, vel propter Monstationem Taurum vel ob Minuem Ducem, vel ut hortaretur vivos ad Agriculturam.

PLUT. *in vita* THESEI. I. 23.

The same Author tells us, that THESEUS's real Father being at first unknown, that Honour was given to NEPTUNE.

Ηο δὲ λογος ὅτι τὰ Πῖδυος Δωιδδις, ὁ, ὁ Πιατειδιοι, τροιαδως, Ππτυβοι γαι ἑ μεξωικα ανδωσι δαγηγδικος, ὁ διας δοξ τεω αιξιη Πλαυχμα, ὁ ὁι σκωσοι αυτηχηδιας, οι ΤΡΙΑΙΝΑΝ ποιησας ιχηση τοι Νεωπωιδω.

Rumor erat per PITTHEA vulgatus esse eum (THESEUM) ex NEPTUNO prognatum; Siquidem colunt eximie *Trozenii* NEPTUNUM, atque est Illic Tutelaris iis Deus, cui Primitias frugum libant, & Tridentem Nummi habent notam. Ib. P. 5.

(2) Τοθτ τολλοις τῶ οι Αθηναιοι Νομισμαι, και μαλιστα θυτε οτι θοι ινχη ΕΝΤΕΤΥΠΩΜΕΝΟΝ. Vetus autem erat *Athenientium* Moneta Bos appellata, eo quod Bovem INSCULPTUM haberct, IX. 61. Hence, says he, the Proverb βοε οπι Ποντου, Βοι in lingua, spoken of such as were bribed to silence: It is very strange, that the learned Cl. SCHREVELIUS should mistake these two Passages in such a Manner, as to give the following Account of the *antient Athenian* Money.

THESEUS *Atheniensis* docuit aurum, argentum & æs eo pondere æstu quo Bovem emere possent, talemque nummum sibi dictum, licet Bovem signatum minime habuerit; ita quoque Ανωθει laminam auri, argenti, Æris, quo dcem boves emere valerent, & ανωθυγυΐσι quæ centum; aut βoi fuisse nummum æreum non cusum, linaiινο argenteum, ανωθυγΐσι aureum.

SPERLINGII. Dissert. de Nummis non cusis. 4to. 1700.

(3) P. 9, Note 5.

(4) Τραζηνιοι Αχαιοι συναισθαι Τυδαρω, Εἴτα παλιν ὁι Αχαιοι γενομαι ηλομαισι τους Τραζηνιους. Achæi simul cum *Trozeniis* habitabant *Sybarim*; Achæi postea majorem in numerum crescentes *Trozenios* expulerunt. ARIST. Pol. V. 3.

(5) See the Sheet of Alphabets published by the ingenious Dr. MORTON.

(6) In the *Mem. de l'Acad. des Inscriptions*, Tom. XXVI. 546. It is said, that in the Ruins of *Ægæ* was found a *Greek* Inscription, where the Name of AURASTUS was written with two Sigmas, of the same Form as on these Medals.

this

this Method, yet they could be no Strangers to it among their *Græcian* Neighbours, among whom it might probably have been continued longer than among the Inhabitants of *Old Greece*, where it was not used in HERODOTUS's Time (1). For we find this Method of Writing from right to left more frequently on the Coins of *Magna Græcia* and of *Sicily*, than of thofe of any other Country; the want of attending to which hath led fome Antiquaries into great Miftakes. The learned Editors of the Medals in the imperial Cabinet at *Vienna*, who firft gave the Public the very ancient and curious Coin of *Sybaris* here exhibited, No. 49, not aware that the two Letters on it TM were to be read backwards, and were the two firft Letters of SYBARITON, afcribe it to the *UMBRI*, a very ancient People of *Italy*; an Opinion adopted alfo in another Treatife by the ingenious M. FROELICH (2), who from this Coin takes upon him to prove, that thefe *Umbri* were the firft People in *Italy* who coined Money. But, having traced this Art in its Rife and Progrefs from *Old Greece* to *Italy*, we will venture to fuppofe, that the *Barbarians* (3) and the *Romans* alfo, whenever they did adopt it, were beholden to their *Grecian* Neighbours, from whom the latter borrowed even the original Device of THRESUS's Money; for, PLINY (4) informs us, that SERVIUS TULLIUS, firft ftruck Brafs at *Rome*, with the Device of an Ox, or a Bull, whence the *Latin* Word *Pecunia*.

BUT as the Manner of Writing from right to left has deceived fome Antiquaries, fo alfo the uncommon Shapes of fome of the Letters on the early Medals of *Pofidonia* have led others aftray. The Medal, No. 61, was exhibited to the Public by the learned S. HAVERCAMP (5), for the firft Time, as he fuppofed; the Infcription on which he read *P O M E S*, and attributed it to *Pontaria*, a City of *Italy*, mentioned by STRABO (6), DION. HALIC. (7) and LIVY (8). But if this learned Perfon could have had an Opportunity of feeing and comparing this Coin with thofe others of the fame Kind here exhibited (9), he would have been convinced of his Miftake; and confidering the Subject for the Sake of which he introduced it, he would have been pleafed to have difcovered on this curious Coin the very ancient Shapes of three Letters of the *Greek* Alphabet.

ON the Medal, No. 29, we find the *Omega* introduced into the Infcription, ftill going from right to left. But as this Medal is taken from GOLTZIUS, and no other has yet been found like it, and poffibly the Ω, by Miftake of the Engraver, may have been

---

(1) If, &c. For Inftances of the Boustrophedon Manner of Writing, fee PAUSANIAS, V. 17 and 25. But particularly CHISHULL's *Antiquitates Afiaticæ*.

(2) Inter vetuftiffimos *Italiæ* Populos, fuiffe *Umbros* veriffimo qui Nummum fignarint, atque præ cæteris figura Bovis, quam alioqui æ primis fuiffe conftat, movet me et Scriptorum & Nummorum fuperftitum auctoritas. — Perveftatâ porro *Umbrorum* Nummos hifce fidem facere colligo e duobus argenteis incufis feu concavis nummis, quorum alter inter Numifmata ryrlaea e'melii Aufbriaci Vindobonenfis jam a nobis eft indicatus, fimul alter, item incufus in *Cæfd* Collegii Arabum. Vindobonenfi S. J. modô, in quibus Bovis fianea ac refpidenti Icon confpicitur. FROELICH *Notitia elementaris Numi Antiqui*. 4to. *Vienna* 1758, P. 18.

(3) Of thefe barbarous Nations we have blotted two Medals here exhibited, No. 18 and 27. They are both of the *Lucanian*

the Conquerors of *Pofidonia*, on which we find a *Greek* Infcription. FESTUS fpeaking of their Neighbours, the *Bratii*, fays, *Brutios Emius dixit Bifingues, quod ufo & Græca lingua fciri fint.*

(4) SERVIUS Rex primus fignavit æs, antea rudi ufos *Roma* Remous tradit; fignta eft Notâ pendum ambi et PECUNIA appellatus. XXXIII. 3.

(5) De voces & voces *Bizarius* apud *Greece* fcriptura & ufu Differtatio. In Sylloge fcriptorum de lingua *Græca*. Vol. I. Ludg. Bat. 1736.

(6) III. 159.

(7) VI. 384.

(8) I. 42, called by LIVY *Œofis Pontia*.

(9) See No. 1, 2, 6, 20, 26, 33, 34, 35, 45.

put

put for an Λ.   We will not, upon its Authority only, determine that the Manner of
Writing from right to left was continued after the Introduction of the long Vowels,
H and Ω, which are said to have been invented by Simonides about five hundred Years
before the Birth of Christ.   Though it has been conjectured that thefe two Letters,
together with the other new ones, Θ, Ξ, Ψ, Φ, X, Ϡ, added to Cadmus's Alphabet, were thus
fashioned, the better to accommodate them to the *Bouftrophedon* Manner of Writing; by
their exhibiting the fame Appearance which ever way they fhould be written.

It will not be fo eafy to find out the Origin of the Symbols which accompanied,
or fucceeded to the Bull on the *Pofidonian* Medals.   In No. 23 NEPTUNE is feen standing
between, what may be called, an Olive Branch on one Side, and a Horfe's Head on
the other; which, probably, allude to the Conteft, already mentioned, between him and
MINERVA.   No. 13 and 14, with the old *Etrufcan* Characters, are given by PASSERIUS
and MAZOCHIUS to *Pofedonia*, and placed among thofe of the earlieft Date, but without
fufficient Authority.   MAGNONIUS, with more Probability, afcribes them to *Plifia*, a
City mentioned by LIVY (1).   The Second of thefe was firft publifhed by AGOSTINO,
Dial. V.   M. PELLERIN has alfo given this Medal more accurately engraven, copied
here, No. 57.   But he does not take upon him to determine to what Place it
belongs.

No. 28, 31, 32 are all fingular Medals from GOLTZIUS, the Second of which is
remarkable on many Accounts, particularly for its being of Gold, being the only one
known of that Metal, belonging to *Pofidonia*.

AFTER the *Lucanians* had conquered the *Pofidonians*, we find their Coins infcribed
ΠΑΙΣ and ΠΑΙΣΤΑΝΟ; and, inftead of NEPTUNE at full length, a Head of him,
only with a Trident on the Reverfe of fome, and of others his Son TARAS on a
Dolphin (2).   This Device was particularly adopted by the *Tarentines* in Honour of their
Founder, TARAS; why borrowed by the *Pæfans* is not fo eafy to fay.   PHILARGYRIUS
indeed, in his Commentary on VIRGIL (3), fays that *Pæftum* was a Colony of the
Tarentines.   JULIUS POLLUX, has a Remark on the Word *Nummus*, and on this Device
common to the *Tarentines* and the *Pæfans*.   He fays, that NOYMOΣ (4) *fhould feem to
be of Roman Origin, but is really Greek, ufed by thofe Dorians who inhabited Sicily and
Italy.   ARISTOTLE, in his Treatife on the Republic of the* Tarentines, *fays, that a Coin
was called by them* NOYMOΣ, *and that it exhibited the Figure of* TARAS *the Son of*
NEPTUNE *carried on a Dolphin.*

---

(1) L. IX. C. 13 and 14.

(2) See No. 41, 43, 47, 51, 52.

(3) ——— Biferique Rofaria Pæfti.

Georg. IV. 119.

Pæftum, civitas Lucaniæ eft.   Hæc Civitas *Pofidonia* dicitur & eft
in agro Salentino Colonia *Tarentinorum*.

(4) Ο δὲ Νουμμος ἄνω μεν ειναι Ρωμαιον τουνομα τω Κερισμασιν επι δ βιβλιοτει,
και των αν Ιταλιαν και Σικελιαν Δωριων· ——— Και Αριστελος εν τη Ταραντινων Πολιτειᾳ
φησι καλεισθαι νομισμα παρ αυτοις νουμμον, εφ ῳ εντετυπωσθαι Ταραντα τον Ποσιδωνος
ΑΔΦ.. επιχουμενι.

Lib. IX. 80.

T

No. 17 has the Device of a Boar, with an Inscription in mixed Characters of the *Greek* and *Roman* Alphabet. The Boar appears also on the Medals No. 12 and 60. This Animal we know was offered in sacrifice to the BONA DEA (1), whose Mysteries, so celebrated among the *Romans*, were by them probably introduced at *Pæstum*. We find this Goddess on the Medal, No. 3, with the Inscription wholly in *Latin* Characters, as it is on the Medals, No. 12 and 60. On which, as also on those No. 7, 8, and 15, are the Names of the Duumviri. These were the principal Magistrates of the Colony, answering to the Consuls at *Rome*, of whom it may be observed, that one of the Names is of a *Roman* Family, the other not to be found in that Number. Thus, on the Medal No. 12, C. COMINIUS is to be found among the former, but not L. ARTUSIUS, whence we may gather, that the Magistrates of *Pæstum* were chosen regularly out of the old Citizens and the *Roman* Colonists, as CICERO informs us was the Case at *Agrigentum* (2).

No. 16 is remarkable as well for the Hexastyle Temple, probably one of those noble ones exhibited in the following Plates, as for the Names C N. C O R. and M. T U C. Patrons of the Colony. These were Patricians of *Rome* to whom the City of *Pæstum* had recommended the Care of its Interests, and who, probably for some very signal Service performed by them, were honoured with the Inscription of their Names, an Honour we find rarely paid to the Patrons of any other ancient City.

A MEDAL very nearly similar to this, is that, No. 57, from M. PELLERIN (3), who very properly expresses his Doubts, that the Letters Q V I should be read *QUIRINUS*, to whom MAZOCHIUS supposes the Temple was dedicated.

ON many of the Medals (4) in this Collection we find the *Cornucopiæ* exhibited, all of which bear a great Resemblance to the Medals of *Thurium* (5), on which, together with the Horn, is the Inscription C O P I A. This singular Name was given to *Thurium* by the *Romans*, after they had sent a Colony hither (6). This Resemblance between the Money of these two Cities should seem to indicate a Correspondence and Connection still kept up between *Thurium* and *Pæstum*. We have already remarked the Resemblance between the ancient Coins of *Sybaris* and *Posidonia*, from which the Inhabitants of the two former were descended.

---

(1) Atque BONAM teneram placent abdomine Porcæ.
                                        JUVEN. II. 86.

(2) Cum *Agrigentinorum* duo genera sint, unum veterum, alterum Colonorum —— Cautum est in Scipionis legibus ne plures essent in Senatu ex Colonorum numero quam ex vetere *Agrigentinorum.*
In Verrem. Lib. II. C. 50.

(3) Premier Supplement, P. 20.

(4) See No. 4, 24, 42, 44, 54, 55, 56.

(5) No. 20, 25, 40.

(6) Οἱ δὲ Ἀναβάντες Συβαρῖται Θουρίους, μετωνόμασαν Κρότωνι τὰς πόλεις.
STRABO, Lib. VI. See also LIVY, XXXIV. 53.

This Name agrees well with the Description given by DIODORUS SICULUS of the Fruitfulness of the Territory of the *Sybarites*, L. XII. 11. and will make us less wonder at the Number of Men, 300000, which took the Field against the Crotonians, mentioned by this Historian and by STRABO. These Accounts should not be too hastily condemned, because they do not correspond with the Observations or Experience we may have been able to form. A very Intelligent Native of *Italy*, in a Work lately published, asserts, that this Country, equal in Superficies to *Great Britain*, contains at present above twice its Number of Inhabitants. See *An Account of the Manners and Customs of* Italy. By JOSEPH BARETTI, 8vo. 1768. Vol. I. P. 123.

I t is remarkable that all the Coins infcribed ΠΑΙΣΤ are of brafs; and though, in deference to the Opinions of fome learned Antiquarians who have confidered this Subject, we have fuppofed that fome of thefe were ſtruck by the *Pæftans,* when fubject to the *Lucanians*; yet we cannot help doubting whether they may not all be referred to the *Roman* Times, after the Defeat of PYRRHUS and the feveral States, *Barbarian* as well as *Greek,* that affifted him. For whilft *Pæftum* was fubject to the *Lucanians,* we fee no Reafon why it might not have continued to have coined Silver Money: But after the Defeat of PYRRHUS, and the immenfe Treafures which the *Romans* then acquired, among other Marks of Conqueft and Superiority, this, of appropriating the Coinage of Silver to themfelves, may be reckoned; whilft the Cities of *Magna Græcia* were fuffered to coin Brafs only; that Metal with which the *Romans* had contented themfelves from the Time of SERVIUS TULLIUS to this Period (1).

To conclude; the Engraver takes this Opportunity to acknowledge the Obligation he owes to the Gentlemen who have affifted him in this Undertaking, and at the fame Time regrets the Injunction he is under of not publifhing their Names: However, he hopes this Silence will be taken as a Mark of his Compliance with their Requeft, and a Teftimony of his Gratitude for their Kind Affiftance.

---

(1) Tum primum Populus *Romanus* Argento uti cœpit. i. e. A. U. C. 484.   Epit Liv. XV.

U

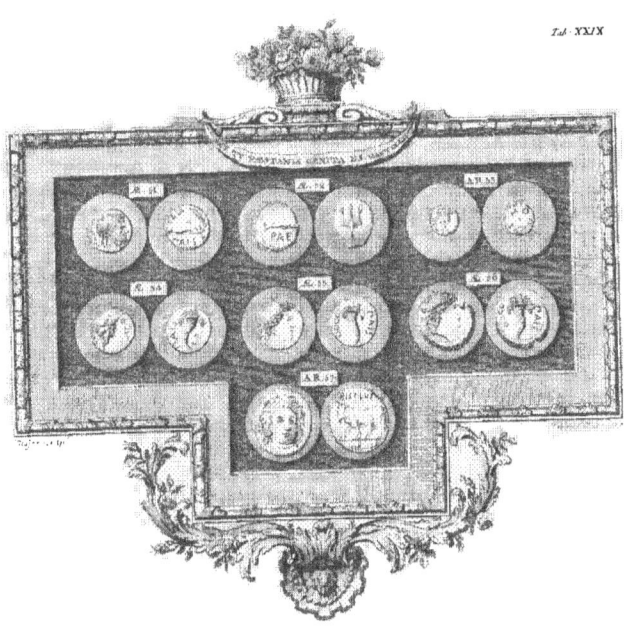

Tab. XXIX

T A B L E

O F

Poſidonian and *Pæſtan* C O I N S,

From whence taken, and in whoſe COLLECTION.

P L A T E XXIV.

No.			No.		
1. DUKE of *Noia* (1)	–	A R	19. Duke of *Noia*	– –	Æ
2. ditto	– – –	A R	20. ditto	– – –	Æ
3. ditto	– – –	Æ	21. MATTHEW DUANE, Eſq;	–	Æ
4. ditto	– – –	Æ	22. ditto	– – –	Æ
5. ditto	– –	A R	23. Earl of *Pembroke*	– –	A R
6. ditto	– – –	A R	24. ditto	– – –	Æ
7. ditto	– – –	Æ	25. ditto	– –	Æ
8. Baron RONCHIUS	–	Æ	26. Duke of *Devonſhire*	–	Æ
9. Duke of *Noia*	– –	Æ	27. PELLERIN	– –	Æ
10. Baron RONCHIUS	–	A R	28. GOLTZIUS	– –	A R
11. ditto	– – –	Æ	29. ditto	– –	A R
12. Duke of *Noia*	– –	Æ	30. ditto	– –	A R
13. Abbé MAZOCHIUS	–	A R	31. ditto	– –	A V
14. ditto	– –	A R	32. ditto	– –	A R
15. Duke of *Noia*	– –	Æ	33. ditto	– –	A R
16. Abbé MAZOCHIUS	–	Æ	34. THESS. BRAND.	–	A R
17. PELLERIN (2)	– –	Æ	35. Imperial Cabinet at *Vienna*		A R
18. ditto	– –	Æ	36. M. MAIER	–	A R

(1) Theſe Medals, from No. 1 to 17 incluſive, with No. 19 and 20, are copied from the Plates added to a little Treatiſe by PASCHALIS MAGNOCIUS, *De vera Poſidonia & Pæſti originibus*, in which the Author concludes, that the Duke of *Noia* in his rich Cabinet of ancient Coins, has about ſeventy *Pæſtan* Medals and almoſt as many *Poſidonian*, and though theſe laſt have not above two or three different Devices, yet they vary from each other in Inſcription, Size, Form of the Letters, or other Particulars ſo much, that it plainly appears they were ſtruck by the *Poſidonians*, in different Ages.

(2) M. PELLERIN, in his firſt Supplement, P. 23, has expreſſed a Deſire of ſeeing all the different Medals of *Pæſtum* collected together, and exhibited at one View. This we have endeavoured to accompliſh, and, with the ſame Modeſty and Diffidence with which that learned Perſon has delivered his Sentiments on this great Variety of curious Ancient Coins, he has given the Public, we beg leave to ſubmit ours alſo to thoſe who are converſant in this Branch of Literature.

X

37.

No.

37. ditto	- - -	A R
38. ditto	- - -	A R
39. ditto	- - -	A R
40. ARIGONIUS	- - -	Æ

P L A T E XXV.

41. ditto	- - -	Æ
42. ditto	- - -	Æ
43. MUSELL.	- - -	Æ
44. ditto	- - -	Æ
45. Capt. JOHN SIVRIGHT	-	Æ
46. ditto	- - -	A R

P L A T E XXVI.

| 47. MATTHEW DUANE, Efq; | - | Æ |
| 48. ditto | - - - | A R |

P L A T E XXVIII.

| 49. Imperial Cabinet at *Vienna* | Æ |

No.

| 50. M. MAÏER | - - - | A R |

P L A T E XXIX.

51. *His Moſt Chriſtian Majeſty*		Æ
52. ditto.	- -	⎫(1)	Æ
53. PELLERIN (2)	- - -	A R
54. Rev. Mr. KAYE	- -	Æ
55. ditto.	- - -	Æ
56. ditto	- - -	Æ
57. PELLERIN	- - -	A R

P L A T E XXX.

58. PELLERIN	- - -	Æ
59. ditto	- - -	Æ
60. ditto	- - -	Æ
61. HAVERCAMP	- -	A R

(1). The Public are beholden to the Generoſity of the learned Abbé BARTHELEMY, for ſending Drawings of theſe Medals to the Engraver, to be inſerted in this Work.

(2) This is the ſmalleſt of the known *Pofidonian* Medals, and is finely wrought for its Size; it weighs but twelve Grains.

EXPLICATION

PLATES.

SEVERAL different Views of each Temple, the moſt pichureſque and agreeable, are exhibited in this Work, as they appeared from the Ruins in 1758, with the Plans and Elevations reſtored, as when they were entire, in order to give the Reader a clear Idea of theſe ancient Buildings.

It muſt be obſerved, that the faint Parts engraved on the Plans, denote what has been reſtored, on a Suppoſition, as nearly as could be determined from the Parts which are now remaining.

N. B. All the Meaſures are in *Engliſh* Feet, Inches and Lines.

PLATE I.

General View of the ruined City of *PÆSTUM*.

A. Hexaſtyle Ipetral Temple.
B. Hexaſtyle Peripteral Temple.
C. Pſeudodipteral Temple, or Baſilica.
D. One of the City Gates.

E F. The City Walls.
F. The Amphitheatre.
G. Rivulet of petrifying Water.

PLATE II.

View of the three Temples taken from the Eaſt (1).

PLATE III.

North View of the City of *PÆSTUM*, taken from under the Gate (2).

PLATE IV.

View of the Gate from within the Wall.

PLATE V.

View of the Gate from without the Walls.

PLATE VI.

Plan of the Hexaſtyle Ipetral Temple.

A. Portico.
B. Pronaos.
C. Naos, or Cella.
D. Poſticus.
E F. Antæ, or Pilaſters of the Pronaos.
F F. Antæ, or Pilaſters of the Poſticus.

G G. Stairs aſcending to the Top of the Temple.
H. Portico of the Back Front.
I I. The lateral Walls of the Temple.
K K. The Line on which the Geometrical Section, Plate XI. is taken.

(1) This View was taken in Preſence of his Excellency Sir JAMES GRAY, and engraved from a fine Painting in the Collection of Major General GRAY.

(2) This View was alſo taken in Preſence of his Excellency Sir JAMES GRAY, and engraved from a fine Painting in his Collection.

View

P L A T E   VII.

View of the Hexaſtyle Ipetral Temple, taken from the South.

P L A T E   VIII.

View of the foregoing Temple, taken from the South-Weſt.

P L A T E   IX.

Internal View of the foregoing Temple, taken from the North.

P L A T E   X.

Elevation of the foregoing Temple reſtored.

P L A T E   XI.

Geometrical Section of the foregoing Temple reſtored, taken on the dotted Line K K. in the Plan, Plate VI.

P L A T E   XII.

Detail of the Members of the foregoing Temple at large, with their Meaſures.

Fig. 1. Capital and Entablature.

Fig. 2. Plan of the Capital.

Fig. 3. Plan of the Column at its Foot.

Fig. 4. Capital and Architrave of the Naos, or Cella.

Fig. 5. Plan of the Capital of the Columns of the Naos.

Fig. 6. Plan of the Foot of the Columns of the Naos.

Fig. 7. Capital and Architrave of the upper Order.

Fig. 8. Plan of the Capital of the upper Order.

Fig. 9. Plan of the Column of the upper Order at its Foot.

Fig. 10. Antæ, Capital, and Entablature of the Pronaos.

Fig. 11. Plan of the angular Modillion, with the Soffita of the Cornice of the Pronaos.

P L A T E   XIII.

Plan of the Hexaſtyle Peripteral Temple.

A. Portico.

B. Pronaos.

C. Naos, or Cella.

D. Poſticus.

E. Portico of the Back Front.

F F. Stairs aſcending to the Top of the Temple.

C G. Antæ of the Pronaos.

H H. Antæ of the Poſticus.

I I. The lateral Walls of the Temple.

P L A T E   XIV.

View of the Hexaſtyle Peripteral Temple.

P L A T E   XV.

View of the foregoing Temple, taken from the North-Weſt.

P L A T E   XVI.

Internal View of the foregoing Temple, taken from the North.

P L A T E   XVII.

Elevation of the foregoing Temple reſtored.

P L A T E   XVIII.

Plan of the Pſeudodipteral Temple or Baſilica.

A. Portico.

B. Naos, or Cella.

C. Portico of the Back Front.

D D. E E. Antæ of the Porticos.

F F. The lateral Walls of the Temple.

P L A T E

PLATE XIX. A.

View of the Pfeudodipteral Temple, or Bafilica, taken from the North.

PLATE XIX. B.

View of the foregoing Temple, taken from the North-Weft.

PLATE XX.

Internal View of the foregoing Temple, with the three Columns ftanding in the Middle, taken from the South.

PLATE XXI.

Internal View of the foregoing Temple, with the three Columns ftanding in the Middle, taken from the North.

PLATE XXII.

Elevation of the foregoing Temple reftored.

PLATE XXIII.

Detail of the Members of the Peripteral and Pfeudodipteral Temples, with their Meafures.

Fig. 1. Capital and Entablature of the Peripteral Temple.

Fig. 2. Plan of the Capital.

Fig. 3. Plan of the Column at its Foot.

Fig. 4. Capital and Entablature of the Pfeudodipteral Temple.

Fig. 5. Plan of the Capital.

Fig. 6. Plan of the Column at its Foot.

Fig. 7. Capital and Entablature of the three Columns ftanding in the Middle.

Fig. 8. One of the Columns of the outer Range, at large.

PLATE XXIV.

Coins and Medals of *Pæftum* or *Pofidonia*.

PLATE XXV.

Coins and Medals of *Pæftum* or *Pofidonia*, ferving as a Head-Piece to the Differtation.

PLATE XXVI.

Coins and Medals of *Pæftum*, or *Pofidonia*, ferving as a Head-Piece to the Enquiry into the Origin of *Pæftum*, or *Pofidonia*.

PLATE XXVII.

View of fome Fragments near the great Temple, ferving as a Head-Piece to the Defcription of the Temples.

PLATE XXVIII.

Coins and Medals of *Pæftum*, or *Pofidonia*, ferving as a Tail-Piece to the Differtation.

PLATE XXIX.

Coins of *Sybaris*, ferving as a Head Piece to the Defcription of the Coins.

PLATE XXX.

Coins or Medals of *Pæftum* or *Pofidonia*, ferving as a Tail-Piece to the Table of Coins.

THE END.

ERRATA.

Page 8, Line 18, for TARENS read TARAS.

Page 13, Line 10, after *Romans*, add, having changed their Language and Cuftoms.

Page 14, Line 26, for *eighteen* read *twelve*.

Page 25, Line 3, for *even* read *perpendicular*.

The WORKS of *T. MAJOR*, Engraver to His Majesty,
taken from capital Paintings in the most eminent Collections of *ENGLAND*
and *FRANCE*; Printed on Grand Eagle Paper, contained in one Volume, or
sold separate, by the Author, in *St. Martin's Lane*, London. 1768.

TITLE of the PRINTS.	Painters Names.	Breadth. Ft. In.	Height. Ft. In.	In whose COLLECTION.
THE Title	Gravelot.	1 3	1 7	
Evening	Berghem.	0 7½	0 6½	
A Sea Piece	B. Peters	1 0	0 10½	Dr. Barnard, Bishop of Derry.
Morning	Berghem	0 7½	0 6½	
A View of the Nordics	Cuype	1 0	0 10½	Sir Luke Chaub, Kt.
Food for the Body	Brower	0 4½	0 7½	Monſ. Goinin.
Food for the Soul	ditto	0 4½	0 7½	ditto
Les Voyageurs	Berghem	1 1½	0 11	Monſ. Le Marquis d'Argenſon.
La Petite Nôce de Village	Teniers	0 10½	0 9½	Monſ. Le Grand.
La Chaſſe aux Oiſeaux	ditto	1 2½	1 0½	ditto
Vue de Canal prôche de Haerlem	Vanderneer	1 0	1 2½	Duke of Montague.
A Landſcape and Cattle	Berghem	2 0	1 8	John Barnard, Eſq;
A Sea Storm	Vernet	2 0	1 8	Mr. Gabriel Mathias, Painter.
Paſſetems Flamand	Teniers	0 10½	0 9	Monſ. Le Blanc.
* Le Jeu de Quilles	ditto	1 2½	1 0	Monſ. de Gagny.
Recreation Flamande	ditto	0 10½	0 9	Mr. Ewer.
* La Moiſſon	Wouvermans	1 2½	1 1	Monſ. Le Brun.
The Death of the Stag	ditto	2 2	1 7½	Comte de Bruhl.
The Laboratory	Teniers	0 11½	1 4	Henry Hoare, Eſq;
The Chymiſt	ditto	0 11½	1 4	Mr. Ford.
The Seaſons, in four Plates	Ferg	0 9	0 8½	Gilbert Earl, Eſq;
The Gravel Pits	Teniers	0 10½	0 8½	Earl of Egremont.
The Sand Hill	ditto	0 10½	0 8½	ditto
Four Romantic Views	Ferg	0 5½	0 8	Mr. Robert Clee.
Jacob's Departure	F. Lauro	2 0½	1 8	H. R. H. the Prſs. Dowager of Wales.
The Miraculous Draft of Fiſhes	Teniers	2 0½	1 8	Boucher Cleeve, Eſq;
The Friendly Invitation	ditto	0 9½	0 7½	John Barnard Eſq;
Vue de Flandre	Rubens	1 2½	1 0	R. Willis, Eſq;
A View of Teniers's Houſe	Teniers	0 7½	0 10	Matthew Duane, Eſq;
Le Calme	Vandervelde	1 3	1 0	Earl of Egremont.
A Sea Piece by Moonlight	Monamy	1 3½	1 6½	B. May, Eſq;
A Flemiſh Wake	Teniers	2 5½	1 10½	Boucher Cleeve, Eſq;
Boy and Goat	Vanderborſch	0 9½	1 1	ditto.
Farm Yard	Hemſkirk	0 9½	1 1	Mr. Burges.
Le Manége	Wouvermans	1 6½	1 1½	Monſ. Le Marquis d'Argenſon.
A View of Blankenburg Caſtle	Vangoen	1 3	1 0	William Herring, Eſq;
Le Chirurgien de Campagne	Teniers	1 7½	1 2½	Monſ. Goinin.
* Les Adieux	Wouvermans	1 6	1 3½	Monſ. Le Chevalier de la Rocque.
A Landſcape and Figures	Teniers	1 7½	1 3½	H. R. H. Frederic Prince of Wales.
Winter Occupation	Berghem	1 4½	1 0½	Lord Viſcount Middleton.
* La Converſation	Teniers	1 5½	1 1½	Earl Temple.
A View of the Port of Leghorn	C. Lorraine	1 6½	1 3½	—— Wiltſhire, Eſq;
A View of the Ponte-Mole near Rome	ditto	1 6½	1 3½	Earl of Aſhburnham.
The Jealous Huſband	Teniers	1 5½	1 2½	H. R. H. Frederic Prince of Wales.
Le Soleil Levant	Vanderneer	1 6	1 1½	Chriſtopher Batt, Eſq;
Clair de Lune	ditto	1 6	1 1½	ditto.
Le Printems, Vue de Rhône	Teniers	1 6	1 1½	Boucher Cleeve, Eſq;
L'Eté	ditto	1 6	1 1½	Earl of Beauſort.
L'Autonne	ditto	1 6	1 1½	Thomas Pratt, Eſq;
* L'Hiver	ditto	1 6	1 1½	Dr. Newton, Biſhop of Briſtol.
A Landſcape and Figures	C. Pouſſin	1 3½	1 2	Mr. Langton.
Ditto its Companion	ditto	1 5½	1 2	Boucher Cleeve, Eſq;
A View of Languard Fort	Gainſborough	2 0½	1 4	Captain Thickneſs.
A View of Harleyford, near Marlow	Zuccarelli	2 0½	1 4	William Young, Eſq;
A Landſcape and Figures	Cuype	1 7½	1 3½	John Barnard, Eſq;
Firſt View in Italy	Vernet	1 8	1 2½	Mr. Gabriel Mathias, Painter.
Second View ditto	ditto	1 8	1 2½	ditto.
Agreeable Solitude	P. Potter	1 4	1 6½	Boucher Cleeve, Eſq;

***** Plates engraved by the late celebrated Mr. Andrew Lawrence.

Tab. 1.

A General View of the Ruined City of Persepolis

A. The Ruins of the principal Palace
B. The principal Stairs and Portals
C. ...
...
G. A View of a Mountain of extraordinary Mass.

Ensemble de la Vue des Ruines de Persépolis

A. Ruines du principal Palais   E. Escalier de la Ville
B. Escalier principal et Portes   F. ...
C. ...   ...
D. Vue du Nord de la Ville   G. Montagne dont la Masse est prodigieuse

View of the three Temples, taken from the East.

Vue de trois Temples, prise du coté de l'Est.

Tab. XI.

A North View of the City of Pæstum: taken from under the Gate.

Vue de Pæstum du coté du Nord, prise de dessous l'Arcade de la Porte de la Ville.

Tab. XIV.

View of the Gate from within the Walls?
Vue de la Porte du Coté de la Ville.

Tab 17

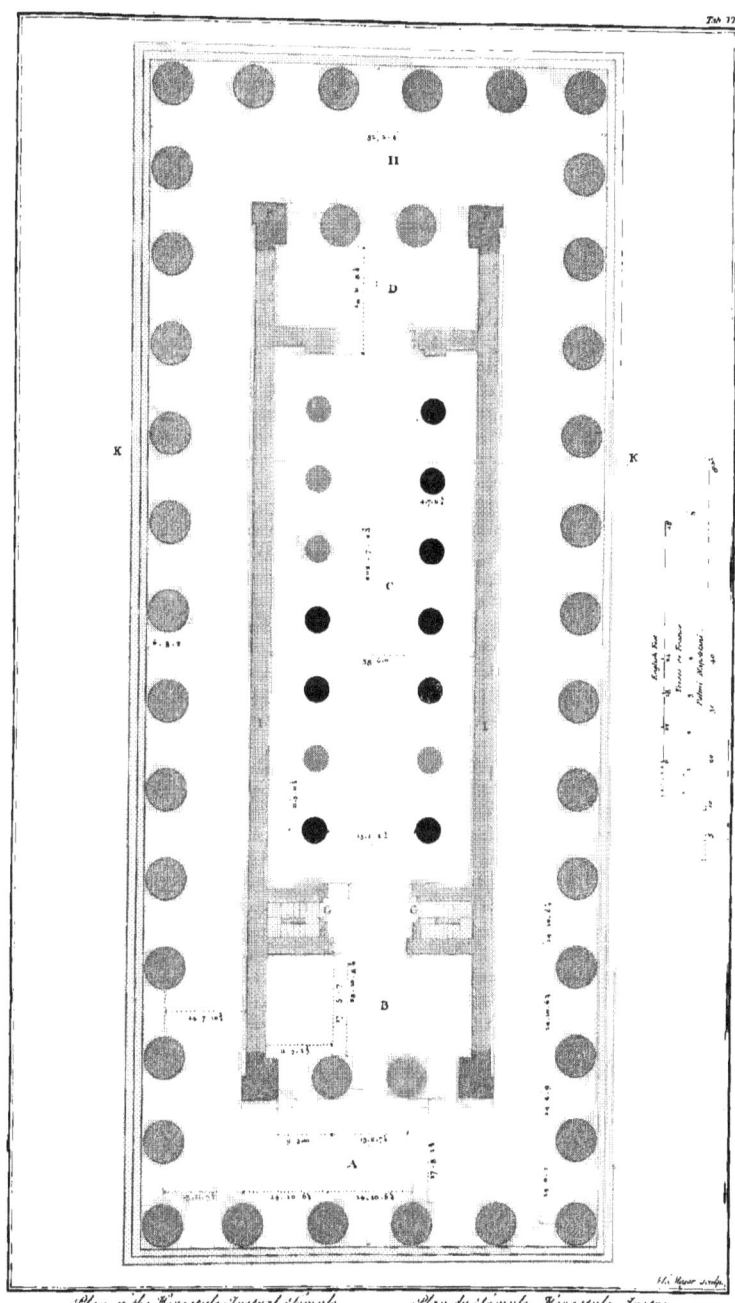

Plan of the Hexastyle Spetral Temple.   Plan du Temple Hexastyle Spetre.

View of the Hexastyle Spetral Temple, taken from the South.

Vue du Temple Hexastyle Spetre, prise du coté du Sud.

Tab. VIII.

A View of the Hexastyle Spetral Temple taken from the South West.

Vue du Temple Hexastyle Spetro prise du coté du Sud Ouest.

Internal View of the Hexastyle Spetral Temple, when from the South
Vue du dedans de Temple Hexastyle Spetre, prise du coté du Sud

Tab. X.

Elevation of the Heitrostyle Systyl Temple.

Elevation du Temple Heitrostyle Systyle.

Tab. XI

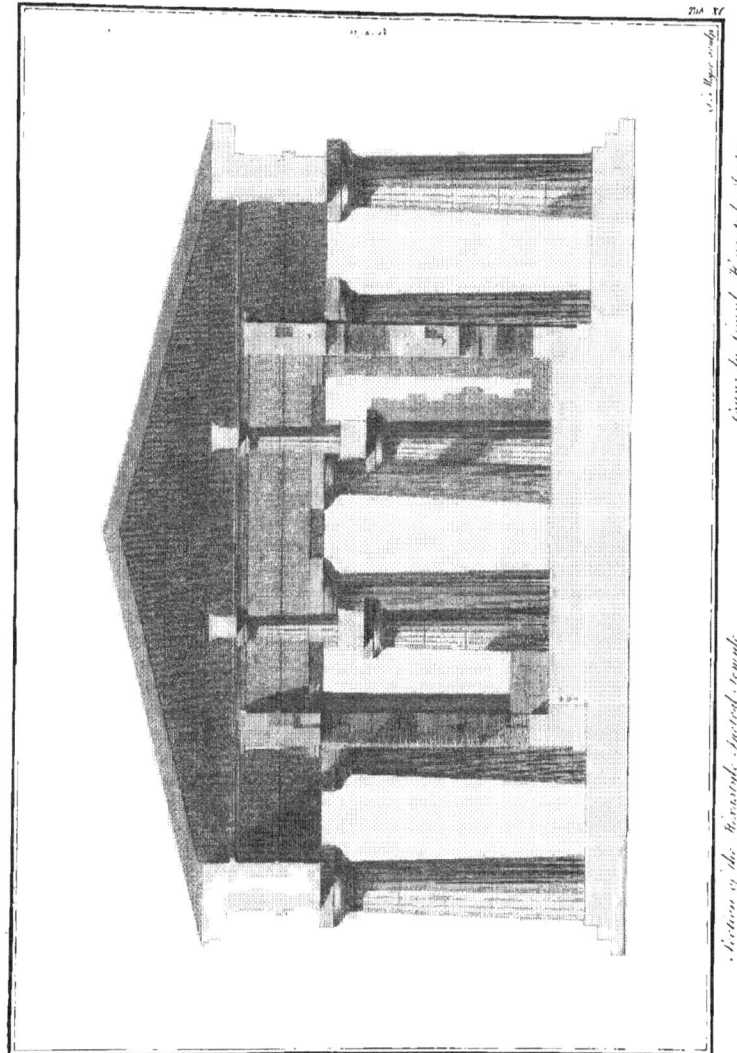

Section of the hexastyle Speudo. temple.

coupe du temple Hexastyle Speudo.

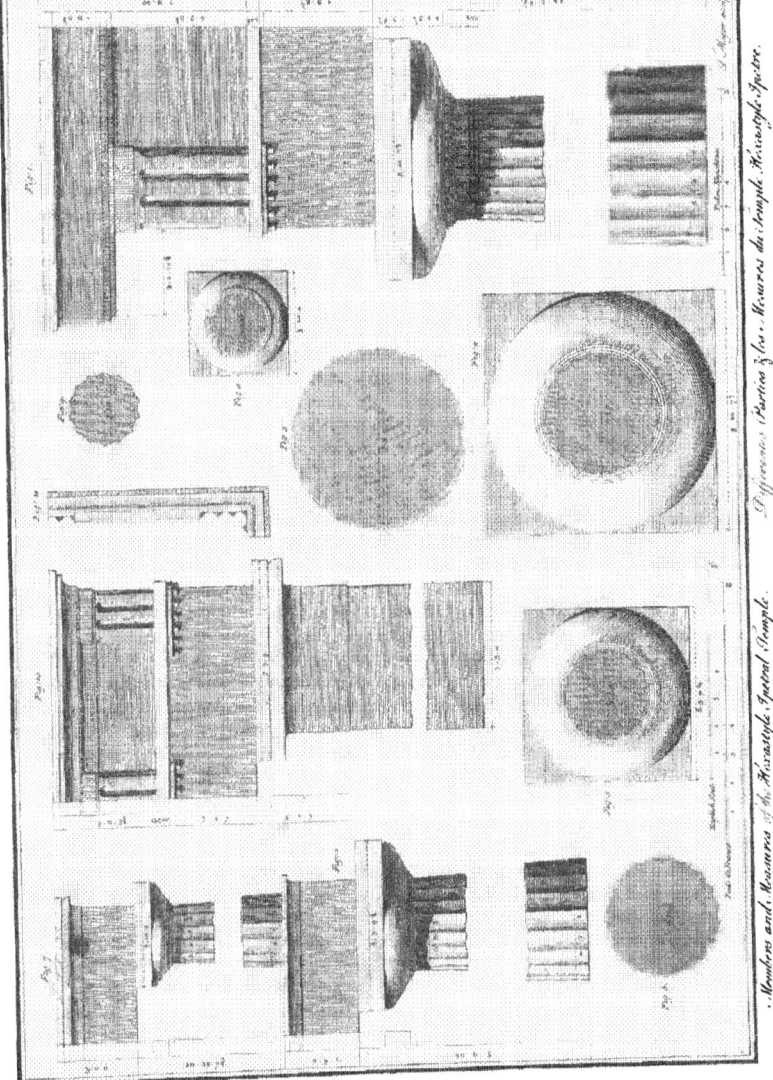

Tab. XII

Members and Measures of the Hexastyle Peral Temple . . . . Differentes Parties et les Mesures du Temple Hexastyle Peptre.

Tab. XXII

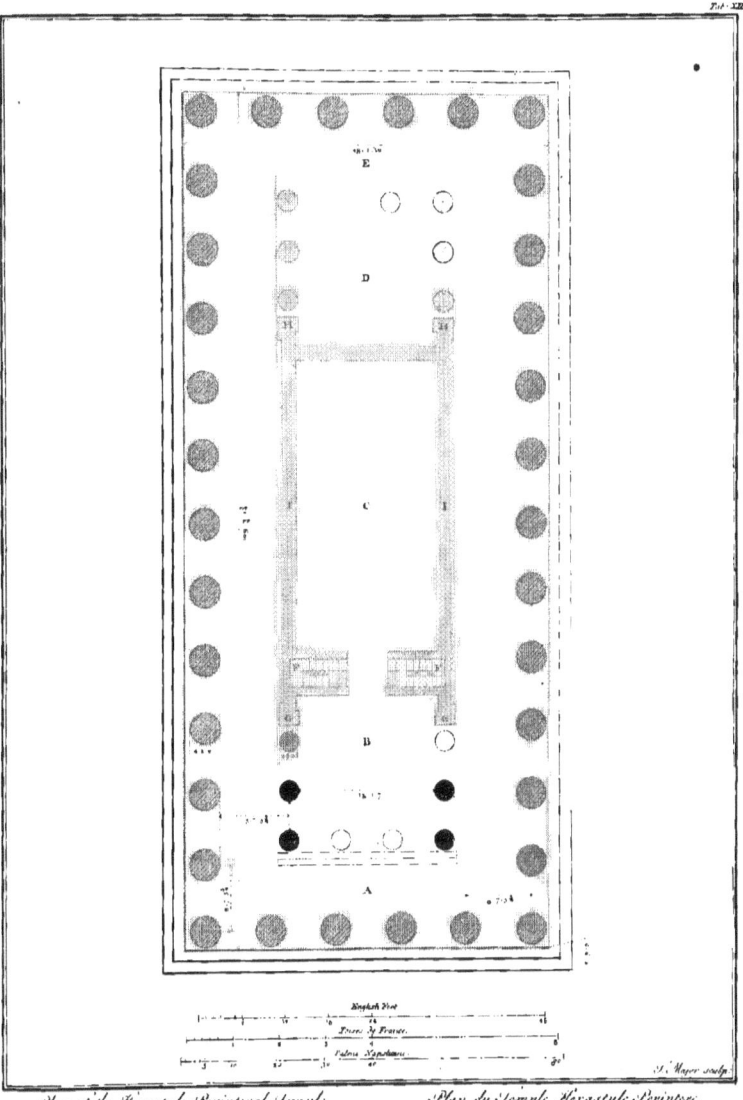

Plan of the Hexastyle Peripteral Temple.   Plan du Temple Hexastyle Periptere.

Tab. XXIII

A View of the Hexastyle Peripteral Temple, taken from the South.

Vue du Temple Hexastyle Periptere, prise du coté du Sud.

View of the Hexastyle Peripteral Temple, taken from the North West.
Vue du Temple Hexastyle Periptere, prise du coté du Nord Ouest.

Tab XVI

Internal View of the Hexastyle Peripteral Temple, taken from the North.

Vue du dedans du Temple Hexastyle Périptère, prise du côté du Nord.

Tab. XVII.

Elevation of the Hexastyle Peripteral Temple.

Elevation du Temple Hexastyle Periptere.

Tab. XVIII

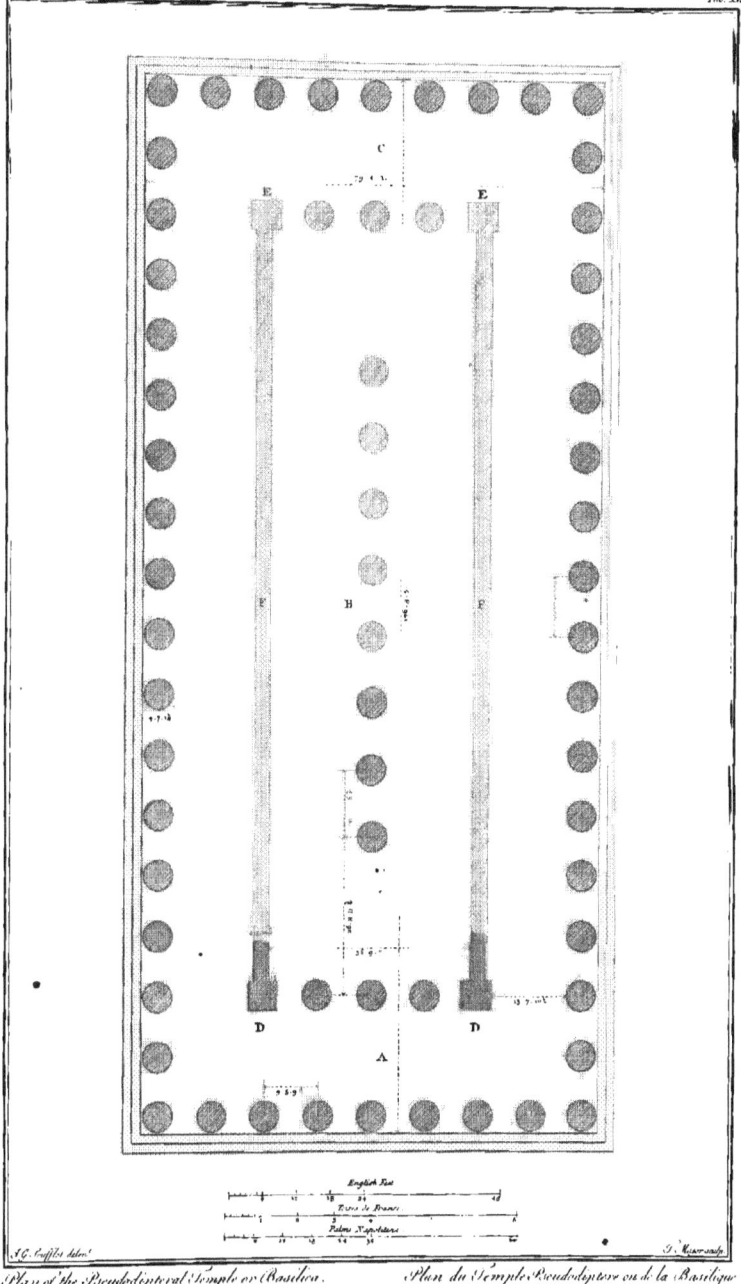

J.G.Soufflot delin.

Plan of the Pseudodipteral Temple or Basilica.   Plan du Temple Pseudodiptere ou de la Basilique

A View of the Pseudodipteral Temple or Basilica, taken from the North.

Vue du Temple Pseudodiptere ou de la Basilique, prise du coté du Nord.

Tab. XIX B

View of the Pseudodipteral Temple or Basilica, taken from the North West.

Vue du Temple Pseudodiptere ou de la Basilique, prise du coté du Nord Ouest.

Tab. XX.

Internal View of the Pseudodipteral Temple or Basilica, taken from the South.

Vue du dedans du Temple Pseudodiptere ou de la Basilique, prise du coté du Sud.

Internal View of the Pseudodipteral Temple or Basilica, taken from the North.

Vue du dedans du Temple Pseudodiptere ou de la Basilique, prise du coté du Nord.

Tab. XXII.

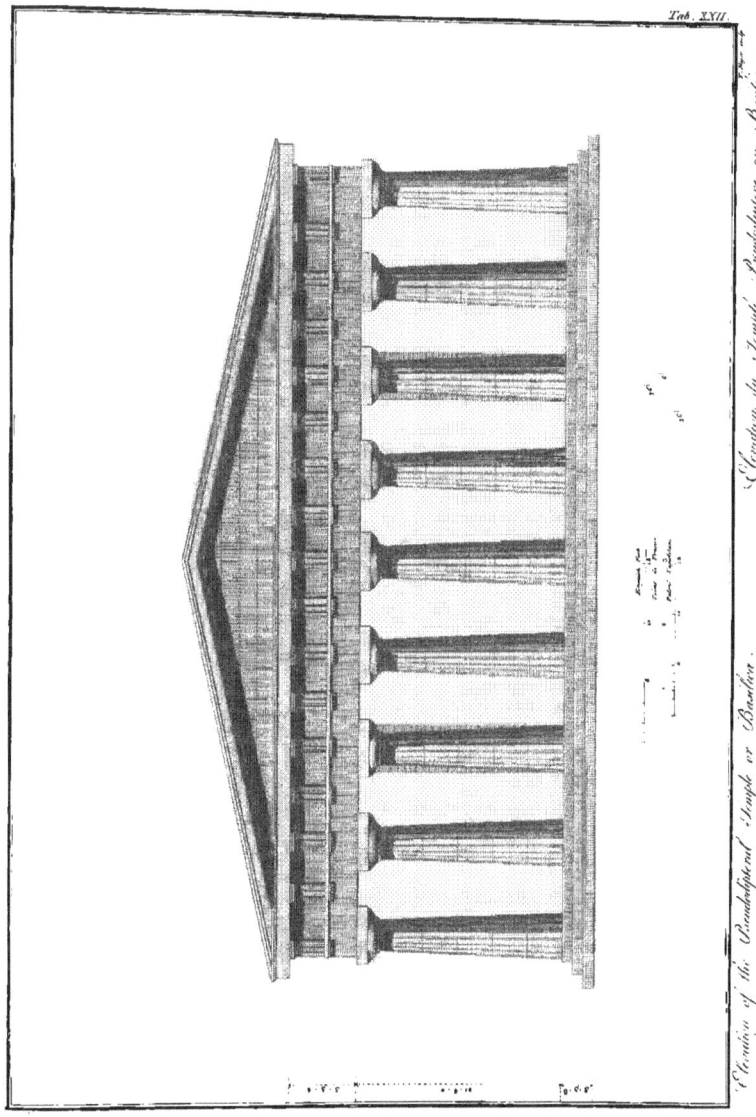

Elevation of the Pseudodipteral Temple or Basilica.   *Elevation du Temple Pseudodiptere ou Basilique.*

Tab. XXIII

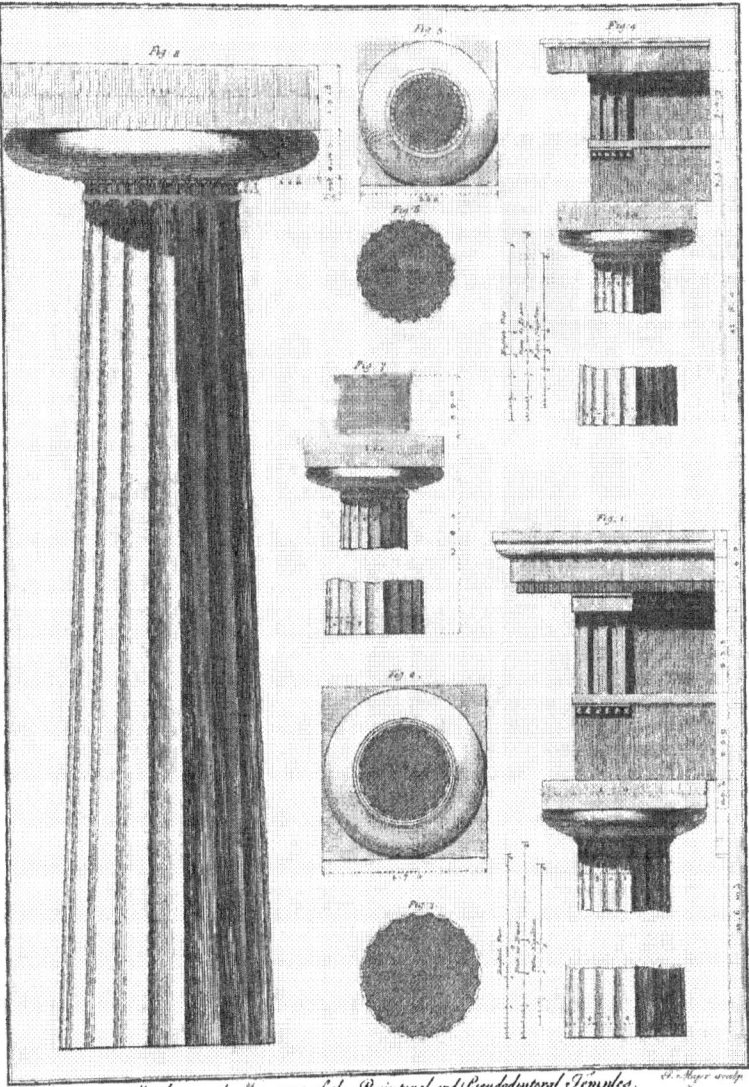

Members and Measures of the Peripteral and Pseudodipteral Temples.
Différentes Parties & les Mesures des Temples Periptere, & Pseudodiptere.

Tab. XXXI.

Coins and Medals of Pæstum or Posidonia.

Monnaies et Medailles de Pæstum ou Posidonie.

www.ingramcontent.com/pod-product-compliance
Lightning Source LLC
Chambersburg PA
CBHW022149020726
47496CB00008B/2635